Aftershock

Aftershock

Collin Wilcox

Random House: New York

This book is
dedicated to
Lee Wright,
friend of
the family

Aftershock

One

For the past several blocks, sensing that the silence suited our mood, we'd made no effort to make conversation. The time was late, almost an hour after midnight, on a Tuesday night. Tomorrow morning we'd both be up early, preparing for our separate day's work. A little wryly, I realized that neither of us had even hinted at the possibility of "my place." I'd known Ann for less than four months. Was complacency already working against us? Or were we just tired after a party that neither of us had enjoyed?

The party had been given by a hip-talking radiologist, recently divorced. Repeatedly, the host had loudly proclaimed himself an ex-friend of Ann's ex-husband. Therefore—now—he was an admirer of Ann's. But Ann's ex-husband had also been a doctor: a sadistic, supercilious society psychiatrist. She didn't like doctors.

Discovering that I was a policeman, the host had immediately become patronizing. All evening he'd quipped about "the police mentality," and "I-can-get-it-for-you-wholesale law." When he also discovered that I'd once played professional football, mostly as a second-stringer, I'd gotten our coats.

"There." Ann pointed to a space between a driveway and a four-door Buick. "Can't you get in there?"

"Maybe." I pulled up, put the car in reverse, and backed until my bumper made gentle contact with the Buick. Moving a few inches forward, I realized that my front bumper overhung the driveway by at least a foot. Shrugging, I switched off the lights and the engine. I wouldn't be long.

She turned toward me, smiling. "I never realized that policemen break so many laws."

"That's because you've never known any policemen." I slipped my right arm around her shoulders. "Have you?"

"You know I haven't." Her clothing rustled as she moved closer. "But I never asked you—how many school teachers have you known?"

"Hmm—" I pretended to think about it, at the same time lightly caressing her hair. The ash-blond hair was soft and fine, exciting to touch. Moving my hand, I traced a slow, sensual line down the curve of her neck, seeking the hollow of her throat. At the touch, she drew a long, lingering breath.

"No fair, Lieutenant Hastings," she whispered. "I've got my children. You've got your career. And it's one o'clock in the morning."

"Hmm—" Moving my hand beneath her chin, I tilted her mouth up to mine. As she kissed me, I felt the lift of her breasts against my chest. Aroused, she was breathing quickly. But finally she drew back, murmuring, "Don't, Frank. We're just making it more difficult."

"It's only five minutes to my place."

"I wouldn't get home until three in the morning. I wouldn't be able to function tomorrow." She wedged a small, determined elbow against my chest and levered us apart. "Teaching fourth grade is nothing like running a squad of homicide detectives, you know. If I'm off my game, they make it miserable for me."

"What about *my* game?"

She smiled. "Which game is that?"

"The game of love. What else?"

"You're very poetic. But you've never faced a classroom of fourth graders."

"True. But I've—"

"Besides, I have a proposition for you."

"Let's take one proposition at a time. We can—"

"Victor is taking the boys to Palm Springs for the weekend. They're leaving Friday afternoon. Did I tell you?"

"You said he *might* be taking them."

"Well, it's definite. And I was thinking—" She hesitated. "I mean, I was talking to Marcie Williamson. And she's going to Portland this weekend. Her mother's sick. So she asked me if I'd like to use her cabin at Stinson Beach."

"And you're asking me."

"Can you get away?"

"Definitely."

With her elbow still firmly wedged, she skeptically smiled. "You've said that before."

"And I always mean it." Making a game of it, I began to draw her toward me, testing her strength.

"I've handled bullies before," she whispered, squirming. "All it takes is a little—"

Suddenly I felt her stiffen. As she'd glanced over my shoulder, her eyes had involuntarily widened.

"What's wrong?" Twisting in the seat, I followed her stare.

"I—" She blinked, then sharply shook her head. "It's nothing, I guess." But still she stared. Across the street the skeletal girders of a large, half-finished townhouse rose two stories high against the sky.

"Did you see something?"

First she sharply shook her head. Then, plainly impatient with herself, she nodded.

"Where?"

"Over there." She pointed to the construction site.

Taking my arm away, I turned to examine the area. Nothing stirred. I turned back to her. My voice dropped to a note of unconscious authority as I said, "What's it all about, Ann?"

"I—I thought I saw someone there—a shadow. Just a shadow."

"Why're you so worried, though?"

"Well, I—" Eyes still straying over my shoulder, she bit her lip. Finally facing me fully, she admitted, "I didn't mention it to you, but lately I—I've had the feeling that someone's been watching me. I've seen—"

"Wait here." I reached across to lock her door, then took my flashlight from its clip beneath the dash.

"Frank. Don't—"

"Just stay put. I'll take a look. Keep the doors locked." Without waiting for a reply, I got out of the car, locked my own door and stood for a moment beside the car, looking and listening. The street was quiet. It was a good, semiaffluent neighborhood. But the ghetto was less than ten blocks away. Street crime was common here.

Walking slowly, holding the unlit flashlight down at my side, I crossed the silent street. On the far sidewalk I paused, standing motionless. From somewhere deep inside the rectangular hatchwork of girders and darkness I heard a small, furtive scrape of movement. I drew my service revolver, careful that Ann didn't see. Slowly, step by step, I moved forward, uncertain of my footing on the debris-strewn ground. What did I expect to find? A dog rooting in the rubble? A prankster? Waywardly, I was thinking that I was doing a patrolman's job —after hours, for love. Literally for love. I was—

Another rustle of movement. Something—someone—was in there. Crouching low, with my revolver in my right hand and the still-darkened flashlight in my left, both probing forward, I was moving close to the concrete foundation buttress, keeping to its shadow. Just ahead I made out the pale oblongs of plywood sheets, lying on the ground. If I walked on the sheets, and they shifted, I would reveal myself. I would . . .

A shadow distorted the geometric symmetry of a thick upright pillar. Instantly I drew back the revolver's hammer, at the same time clicking on the flashlight. "Hold it right there."

Leaping, the figure of a man vaulted a low wall, tumbling on the far side. Gone. As he'd leaped over, I'd seen the unmistakable outline of a gun clutched in his right hand—a sawed-off-shotgun shape. A submachine-gun shape.

Clicking the flashlight off, I was scrambling for the pillar he'd just left. My feet slid wildly on the plywood oblongs. Falling to one knee on the wood, I heard fabric rip. It was my newest suit. Two hundred dollars. Up again, jinxing, I dodged behind the pillar, safe.

Would a blast from his gun rip through the darkness?

Panting, fighting the throat-clogged hammering of my heart-beat, I looked quickly back to my car. Inside, I could see Ann's head. Could she see me? Had she heard the chase—seen his gun? Desperately, I willed her to go into her flat, call Police Dispatch, send me help. But I'd told her to stay inside the car, doors locked. I'd . . .

From the far side of the low wall came a soft, furtive scuttle of movement, drawing away. He was frightened, then—ready to run. I should let him go. Without reinforcements, I should let him go.

But, silently, I was stepping away from the safety of the pillar. Bent double, head below the level of the wall, I was duck-waddling toward the movement I'd heard. The sound had come from the far end, where the wall joined the foundation buttress. Deliberately, I scraped my feet, making noise. If I could . . .

Footsteps were running, leaving the wall, escaping. I placed my flashlight on top of the wall, vaulted over, grabbed the flashlight.

"Police officer. Halt, or I'll fire."

I saw his shadow wildly running. Momentarily his silhouette was streetlight-limned. I could see both his arms, flung wide as he ran. I could clearly see his hands, empty. Straightening, I was running—fighting for footing in the debris. He was . . .

The running silhouette pitched forward, falling heavily. I heard him grunt, then softly swear. A dozen strides, and I was standing over him. In the glare of my flashlight beam his eyes were wild.

"Roll over." Easing the revolver's hammer off, I jammed the barrel into his neck, below the ear. "*Now.*"

"Don't shoot. I haven't done anything."

"You've got a gun. Where is it?"

"*What* gun?" His anguished voice was high, fear-cracked. "Roll over."

When he obeyed, I jammed my knee in the small of his back, slipped my revolver into my waistband and quickly cuffed him. "All right. On your feet." I jerked him up, shining the light full in his face.

"What're you *doing*, anyhow?" he shrilled. Standing with spindly legs braced wide, he tossed his greasy, half-long hair back from his eyes. He was in his early twenties. He wore faded Levi's and a torn leather jacket, mud-stained down the front. His twitching face was blotched and pale; his eyes blinked away from the flashlight, their pupils enlarged. He was a junkie.

Holstering my gun, slipping the flashlight into my jacket pocket, I glanced back over my shoulder. Ann was still inside the car. On the street nothing stirred. The brief, silent chase had gone unnoticed. We were standing close beside a tall pile of lumber, still metal-banded. Suddenly I grabbed the front of his jacket, jamming him back against the wood. His head bounced—once, twice. His protests were rattling in his throat, suddenly panic-choked.

"Where's the goddamn gun?" I sunk my fingers into his exposed throat.

"It wasn't a gun. There's no gun."

"What'd you have in your hand, then?"

Desperately shaking his head, eyes wild, he began to sob.

"All right," I said. "It's your ass. What's your name?"

"Bl—Blake. Sonny Blake."

"You're going to spend the night in jail. Do you know that, Sonny?" As I spoke, I relaxed my grip on his throat. He sagged toward me, almost falling. I turned him around, pushing him toward the street. "All right, walk." I hooked the fingers of my left hand into the handcuffs. "Slow and easy, Sonny." With my right hand I drew the flashlight, searching the littered, mud-puddled ground as I walked. I saw a short length of conduit, but no gun. Could it have been the conduit that I'd seen? Was I arresting a harmless vagrant? It had happened before.

I threw him into the back of my car and watched him while Ann called Dispatch. A black-and-white car arrived in minutes. I ordered that Blake be booked and that the construction site be searched for a gun the next morning. I watched the patrol car clear the area. Then I softly knocked on Ann's front door.

"Come in the living room," she whispered. "I don't want to wake the children." She was still wearing her coat, but she'd slipped off her shoes. Her eyes were wide and somber.

I followed her into the living room and sat close beside her on the couch, taking her hand. She'd lit a single lamp, dim in a far corner. Like a frightened child's, her fingers worked within mine, seeking silent comfort.

"Have you ever seen him before?" I asked quietly.

"No. Wh—who is he, Frank?"

"His name is Sonny Blake. To me, he looks like a small-time hustler. Possibly a drug addict."

"But what does he want?" As she asked the question, her voice faltered.

"I don't think it's anything serious, Ann. Are you absolutely sure somebody's been watching you?"

"Well—" She hesitated. "It's been more of a feeling, I guess. But last week Billy said that he saw someone looking over the back fence."

"Billy's only ten, Ann."

"I know. Still . . ." Suddenly she shivered, snuggling closer.

"Did Billy describe the person he saw?"

"Yes. Vaguely. And—" She bit her lip. "And it fits this Sonny Blake, Frank. Dirty-looking, longish brown hair, slim."

"Did Billy see him more than once?"

"No."

"Did anyone else see him?"

"I—Marcie might have. When we were talking about my taking her cabin this weekend, she mentioned that she saw someone in the parking lot at school, watching me."

"Same description?"

She nodded. Her eyes had fallen, fixed on my trousers. "You're all muddy," she said. "And your pants are torn."

"I know." I put my arm around her shoulder. "I don't want you to worry about this, Ann," I whispered. "It's nothing. We're going to check it out—make certain. But I can tell you—it's nothing."

Meekly, she nodded. "Yes." Her eyes were still cast down.

Speaking firmly, I said, "I'm going home. You'll be all right. To make sure, I'll have a radio car check the house. Tomorrow morning, first chance you get, I want you to call me at the office. Will you?"

I could feel her gathering herself. "Yes," she answered steadily. "Yes, I'll call you."

Together we rose. Side by side, with our arms circling each other's waist, we walked through the dimly lit entryway to the front door. Gently, chastely, we kissed goodnight, then gravely looked at each other, at arm's length.

"I saw you fighting with him, Frank," she said finally. "I saw you throw him against that stack of lumber." Her eyes faltered, then fell. "It—it frightened me. The violence, I mean. It frightened me. Do you"—she raised her eyes, mutely pleading—"do you know what I mean?"

"Yes," I answered softly, "I know what you mean. I know exactly what you mean."

"I—I'm sorry. I know you—you did it for me."

I considered a moment, still holding her. Then, speaking deliberately, I said, "I only did it partly for you, Ann. Partly I did it because it's my job. It—it's not something I can really explain. But it's my job."

Still with her eyes raised, seeking mine, she said softly, "I can't explain it, either. My—my reaction, I mean. That's what I can't explain."

Not replying, I took her face in both hands, kissing her. "You go to sleep now. Have a brandy and go to sleep. Don't worry. And remember, phone me in the morning, between classes. Promise?"

She promised. We kissed one last time, then said goodnight.

Two

As I unlocked my office door the next morning, I heard the clump of a familiar step behind me. Turning, I saw Pete Friedman, my senior co-lieutenant. Pointedly, he glanced at his watch as he motioned me into my own office with the long-suffering gesture of a grammar school teacher shooing his flock ahead. "It's lucky," he said, "that one of us is an early riser."

"I didn't get home until two o'clock," I objected, slipping into my swivel chair and motioning him to a seat across the desk.

"You look it." He levered his two hundred forty pounds from one side to the other, grunting as he searched first for a cigar, then for matches.

"I read not too long ago," I said, "that Freud got cancer of the jaw from smoking cigars."

"Don't worry about it," Friedman grunted, lighting the cigar. "I'm Jewish, too."

"What's *that* supposed to mean?"

"It means that lots of Jews have a death wish. Else why would I be a policeman?" He shook out the match and threw it, still smoking, into my wastebasket. As I leaned over my desk to stare at the basket, Friedman settled himself in his chair, gratefully sighing. It was Friedman's contention that my visitor's armchair fitted him better than his own—accounting, doubtless, for his constant presence across my desk, squinting

9

at me through a perpetual cloud of cigar smoke as he laconically made plans. Friedman was the homicide squad's strategist—its inside man. I operated in the field.

"I see what you mean about death wishes," I said, still eyeing the wastebasket. "Death by burning."

"Don't worry," he replied. "You won't be around long enough for the fire."

I decided simply to wait, perversely declining the gambit. Announcing some new development, Friedman took a cat-and-mouse pleasure in building the suspense. The script seldom varied. Receiving the call on a homicide that involved more than the usual drunken Saturday-night domestic bludgeoning, or a mugging that turned into murder, Friedman invariably came down the corridor to my office, slumped into my armchair and lit a cigar. Then he began dropping hints.

"We have a homicide in affluent Sea Cliff," he said finally. "Don't take off your coat."

Nodding, I reached for a notepad.

"The victim is one Flora Esterbrook Gaines, female Caucasian, age seventy. Address, 1376 Sea Cliff Avenue."

"When did it happen?"

"Just a little after midnight, last night. It seems to be a robbery-and-murder thing. But since the victim pays—paid—more in annual property taxes than the combined value of our two salaries, the department naturally wants to put on its best, most convincing full-dress performance. Provided, of course, you're up to it after your exertions last sight, collaring Sonny Blake." He paused, puffed on the cigar and eyed me with sidelong speculation. "It doesn't look right," he said finally, "for someone of your rank and position to collar petty hoods single-handedly. It sets a bad example, especially for those of us who are, ah, a little out of condition. I just thought I'd mention it."

"Where's Sonny Blake now?" I asked, at the same time wearily riffling through the stack of interrogation reports awaiting my initials.

"He's in a holding cell. What happened, anyhow?"

Briefly, I told him. As he listened, an inch-long ash fell from Friedman's cigar, bounced off the mound of his stomach and dropped to the floor. Absently brushing at his vest—succeeding only in smudging the ash stain—he said, "Do you want me to interrogate Sonny Blake for you?"

"If you want to. I don't think—" My phone rang. I answered impatiently, then listened as an unfamiliar voice said, "This is Patrolman Les Matthews, Lieutenant. I was ordered, first thing this morning, to make a search of the construction site in the nineteen-hundred block of Buchanan, looking for a possible ditched gun. I was told that I should report to you."

"That's right, Matthews. Did you find anything?"

"We didn't find a gun, Lieutenant. But we did find what appears to be a shotgun mike."

"*What?*"

"That's right, sir. We found it down in a pile of scrap lumber, just beside the north wall of the foundation."

"Are you sure it's a shotgun mike?"

"Well, I'm no electronics expert. But that's what it looks like to me. Do you want us to bring it down to the Hall?"

"Yes," I answered slowly. "Bring it up to Homicide. Give it to Lieutenant Friedman if I'm not here."

"Yessir."

As I hung up, I saw Friedman studying my puzzled frown. "What's it all about?" he asked.

"Apparently," I said slowly, "Sonny Blake was carrying a shotgun mike last night. I thought it was a gun."

For a moment he didn't reply, thoughtfully staring off across the office. Then, musing, he said, "Since I arrived at least an hour before you did this morning, I thought I'd do you a favor and ask Blake a few questions."

"And?"

"And I wonder what a small-time junkie hustler hoodlum is doing with a shotgun mike. Considering that he must've paid several hundred dollars for it."

"Maybe he stole it."

"Maybe," Friedman answered doubtfully. For a moment he was silent. His smooth, swarthy face was utterly impassive. With his chin sunk deep into his jowl-mashed collar, he sat motionless as a buddha. I knew that mannerism; I recognized the inscrutable blankness in his dark, heavily lidded eyes. Friedman was concocting a theory.

"Well," I asked shortly, "are you going to tell me, or not? Flora Esterbrook Gaines is waiting."

Reluctantly, Friedman sighed. "Let me kick this around a little with Sonny Blake. Let's see what I can—"

"Come on, Pete. If there's anything to all this—if Ann is really being followed, I want to know about it. And I want to know now. I can tell by looking at you that—" I broke off, struck by a sudden thought. Watching him closely, I asked, "Does this have anything to do with the Frazer thing? James Biggs?"

"It could be," he answered slowly, finally lifting somber eyes to meet mine. "When you start talking about electronic surveillance equipment and kinky behavior, I start thinking about James Biggs. And, furthermore, I—"

My phone was ringing. I answered brusquely.

"It's Ann, Frank."

"Oh. How are you?"

"Fine. Are there—any developments? You told me to call you, remember? I hate to bother you. Are you busy?"

"A little," I admitted. "Are you going right home from school today?"

"Yes."

"All right. I'll call you at home. You haven't been—worried, have you?"

"A little," she admitted hesitantly. "But there haven't been any more—incidents."

"There won't be, either," I answered firmly. Then, quickly, I said good-bye. I turned to Friedman. "What were you going to say," I demanded, "about James Biggs?"

"Look, Frank, let me see what I can—"

"I want to know." Saying it, I dropped my voice to a low, level note, holding his eye as I spoke. "I'm just not going to sit still for any more of this freeze-out, Pete, and you may as well know it right now. I'm sick of it. I've had it."

For a moment he didn't reply. Then, speaking slowly and seriously, he said, "It's the captain's orders, Frank. You know it just as well as I do. And he got his orders from up top. *Way* up top."

"I don't give a damn. I'm not guilty of a thing. *Nothing*. I know it. Captain Kreiger knows it. Everybody. And I'm just not going to—"

"Don't forget me," Friedman said quietly. As he spoke, he met my eyes squarely. "I know it, too."

For a moment our eyes silently locked. Then, exclaiming impatiently, I banged my palm down on the desk, hard. "I'm not saying you don't," I muttered. "I'm just saying that I'm tired of being treated like a—an idiot child who has to be protected from himself. That's about what it amounts to, you know. Just because the city attorney gets a wild hair up his . . ."

"Listen," Friedman said, raising a broad, beefy hand, "go out and take a look at the Flora Esterbrook Gaines thing. Get some air. I'll talk to Sonny Blake again, and I'll talk to the captain. I'll also detail a cruiser to follow Ann home from school and stake her place out. Meanwhile, cool off. You strong, silent types are all the same. Whenever you think someone's doing something for you, there's a big sweat. And for what? You're—"

"Listen, Pete, I don't like all this crap about Ann's being under some kind of surveillance. And if you're honest, you'll admit that it's just the kind of thing that James Biggs could be involved in. So don't—"

"That reminds me," he interrupted blandly. "Clara told me to tell you that you and Ann can come over for dinner on Saturday night. Clara's sister and her husband are coming, too —from Houston. I don't think we'll get many laughs, because my brother-in-law is a pompous son of a bitch. But, at least, we're having roast beef."

I sighed, locked my desk and rose to my feet, at the same time picking up the slip of paper with the Sea Cliff address. "I can't," I said, turning to the phone. "Ann and I are going away for the weekend. Her husband's taking the kids to Palm Springs. Sorry."

He shrugged. "Don't be sorry. You'll have a better time, no question."

I picked up the phone, got Canelli and told him I'd meet him in the garage. As I was speaking on the phone, Friedman heaved himself to his feet and we walked together to the elevators.

"Don't forget," I said, "you're going to talk to the captain."

"I won't forget." Friedman spread his hands in a plaintive gesture of broadly burlesqued Jewish pique. "Don't worry, I won't forget."

Three

"Where to, Lieutenant?" Canelli slammed his door and started the engine.

"Thirteen seventy-six Sea Cliff Avenue."

"Right." Canelli shifted to reverse, gave the car too much gas and killed the engine. He shot me a sheepish glance as he restarted the engine—after prolonged starter-grinding. I sighed, looking away. Canelli was at perpetual odds with almost everything mechanical. He'd been my driver for six months, a fact that provided Friedman with endless material for lunch-table humor. Why, Friedman wondered, would I pick a driver who had difficulty backing out of a parking stall? How, Friedman asked, could I listen to Canelli's perpetually bemused platitudes?

My defense was always the same—a counterattack. Why had Friedman tapped Canelli for inspector, a little more than a year ago? Simple, came the inevitable rebuttal. Canelli neither looked like a detective nor acted like a detective nor thought like a detective. Therefore, Canelli had been in constant demand as an undercover man, a role that allowed him to sometimes accomplish miracles, otherwise known as Canelli's luck. Success hadn't changed Canelli. At twenty-eight years old, he weighed a suety two hundred forty pounds and waddled when he walked. His suits always bagged and he never creased his hat in the same style twice. For eight years he'd been engaged to the same girl, and he still blushed whenever someone asked about her. On the job his expression alternated between puzzlement, surprise and a deep, lip-chewing concentration. Canelli was the only cop I'd ever known who could get his feelings hurt.

"Is this that old woman?" Canelli asked, elaborately checking traffic before venturing out of the garage and into the traffic stream.

"That's right," I answered. "Her name is Flora Esterbrook Gaines."

"That's some name," Canelli observed. "I hear she's rich."

"Yes."

We drove for a few blocks in silence. Then, tentatively, Canelli said, "I, ah, hear you collared some weirdo last night, Lieutenant."

Again I sighed. Canelli was probing. He had, no doubt, been primed by the other members of the homicide squad to discover why Sonny Blake was under wraps, not to be questioned by anyone except Friedman or myself. Of course, already the squad members would have guessed at the same connection Friedman suspected. But, by training, a detective doesn't like to guess.

We drove for a few more blocks without talking. Finally Canelli frowned. Transparently pretending to be struck by a random thought, he asked, "How're you doing with that Nancy Frazer thing, Lieutenant? I mean, when's it coming to trial?"

"As a matter of fact," I said, "it's scheduled for trial in a couple of months." I paused, eyed him silently for a moment, then said, "Any more questions?"

He glanced at me quickly before shrugging his beefy shoulders. "It's just that I never got that Frazer thing straight," he said, returning his eyes to the road. "I mean, it all happened before I made inspector, you know. It must've been, lessee—" He elaborately wrinkled his brow. "It must've been two years ago now. Mustn't it?"

"Just about two years," I answered. Then, curious to know what he'd actually discovered, I said, "What'd you hear about the Frazer thing, Canelli?"

"Well—" Again he shrugged, diffidently flip-flopping his

hand. "I just heard that there was this shoot-out, and Nancy Frazer got shot by accident. But I never really knew much about it. Plus, there was never much said in the squad room. So I figured that . . ." Having talked himself into a corner, he frowned heavily, concentrating on the road ahead.

"You figured that the lid was on."

Uncomfortably, he nodded. "Something like that, I guess."

"And the characters in the squad room want to know what's happening. Is that it?"

"Well, jeeze, Lieutenant, I wouldn't want you to think I'm prying, or anything."

I allowed a long, sadistic moment of heavily laden silence to pass before I said, "Actually, the story's very simple, Canelli. Would you like to hear about it?"

"Well, jeeze, Lieutenant, like I said, I wouldn't want you to think that . . ."

"What happened, three officers and myself—two cars—were chasing a suspect's car down Geary Boulevard. It was almost exactly two years ago. We were just setting up a blockade when the suspect suddenly pulled over to the curb. In fact, he collided with a muni bus. He got out of his car and started running. It was about four P.M., and the sidewalks were crowded. The suspect had a gun, but at first he didn't fire. He just ran. I was teamed with Culligan on foot. The two other officers drove on ahead, trying to head the suspect off at Geary and Arguello. But suddenly the suspect started firing. We scattered, taking cover. The suspect fired twice. We fired a total of five shots. Two officers fired twice, Culligan fired once. I didn't fire. After our five shots, the suspect threw down his gun and gave up. No sweat. Except—" I sighed, suddenly surrendering to the memory of that moment, still so clear in my memory. "Except that one of our bullets caught a bystander. Nancy Frazer. It lodged in her spine and paralyzed her."

"But how come they're hauling you into court, Lieutenant? If you didn't fire your gun, I don't see how—"

"There was no way of determining whose gun fired the crucial shot. It was a ricochet and the bullet was ruined. So since I was in command, I'm the one they're suing. Me, and the city of San Francisco."

"But they can't make it stick, Lieutenant. No way."

I shrugged. "We won't know that until the jury comes in, Canelli. But the plaintiffs are charging negligence. We didn't take proper precautions, they say."

"Well, crap on them."

I ruefully smiled. "Thanks, Canelli. You're a big help."

He looked at me doubtfully, frowned, then asked, "What happened next, Lieutenant?"

"A civil suit was filed on behalf of Nancy Frazer and her son, James Biggs. Biggs was seventeen at the time, and away at school. They waited six months to determine whether she'd be permanently paralyzed. Then they filed."

"What about the husband? Didn't he want a piece of the pie?"

"Apparently not. His name is Chester Frazer. He's her third husband, and he's got enough money, apparently."

"It figures," Canelli said morosely. "So what happened then, Lieutenant? I know she died about six months ago."

"The victim apparently started to drink after the shooting. Maybe she drank before; I don't know. Anyhow, about six months ago she died of a barbiturate overdose—a bad reaction between liquor and drugs. Which is, of course, very common."

"I heard that James Biggs had something to do with her death."

"She probably got the extra barbiturate from him—enough to kill herself. If he provided that barbiturate, knowing that she'd use it to kill herself, then he's involved in her death. Which means that, regardless of whether he's indicted, he's undoubtedly lost any claim of damages against us."

"So that's good. You're a winner, Lieutenant."

"Maybe. But, like I say, you never know until the jury comes in. However, this son is very strange—very neurotic. I've never actually talked to him—I'm *forbidden* to talk to him, in fact. But I understand, from Lieutenant Friedman, that he's a nut. I also understand that he's out to get me. So I'm—"

"Why can't you talk to him?"

"Because it would appear as if we're harassing him, according to the city attorney. I gather that Biggs's lawyers are going to contend that Biggs is a victim of a kind of municipal conspiracy."

"Municipal conspiracy?" He braked the car and turned through the ornate flagstone pillars that marked the entrance to Sea Cliff.

"The coroner's jury ruled that her death was probable suicide. That's going to make it hard for Biggs to collect, whether or not he supplied her with an overdose. So Biggs's lawyer is claiming that the verdict was a put-up job. And, if we give Biggs a hard time, it might look to the jury like the lawyer has a point. First the coroner's jury, then us."

"Yeah," Canelli answered slowly, "I see what you mean. Still, if we could prove that Biggs killed his mother, then you'd *really* be a winner, Lieutenant. Two for the price of one, you might say."

"Never mind the bargains, Canelli. I'll settle for a straight deal. One for one." I pointed ahead. "There it is. That big Spanish-style house, across the street."

"Jeeze," Canelli marveled, pulling to the curb. "That's some place. That's *really* some place."

Four

"This is where they found her," Culligan was saying, pointing to the chalked outline of a body. We were in a spacious three-car garage, all of us facing a tape barrier the crime lab had strung around the murder area. The body had fallen close to the rear wall of the garage, between a Ford station wagon, on the left, and a silver-gray Cadillac, in the center. A Porsche Targa was parked in the right-hand space. Blood was every-where—pooled on the floor, spattered on the garage's rear wall, sprayed on the hood and grille of the Cadillac.

Standing beside me, Canelli muttered, "This has got to be the fanciest garage in town. It looks like a—a men's room, or something, it's so clean."

Culligan turned to stare at Canelli. Tall, gaunt and short-tempered, Culligan was Canelli's exact opposite. Culligan suf-fered from ulcers. His cheeks were hollow, his eyes sunken. His mouth was perpetually turned down, as if he were tasting something sour. Culligan studied Canelli for a long, dead-eyed moment. Then, speaking in his dry, rusty voice, Culligan said, "I guess that depends on the kind of men's room you're used to using." As Canelli frowned, puzzled, I turned to Cul-ligan.

"What's the sequence of events?" I asked.

"Well, of course," Culligan said defensively, "I haven't got it all pieced together. I've only been here for a couple of hours, you know. And all I did last night was make sure everything was secured."

Accustomed to Culligan's wary caution, I nodded. "Just give me your opinion, then."

"Well, the way it looks to me," he said, "she drove up to the garage a little after midnight, last night. She used her electronic door opener, probably without getting out of the car. She drove into the garage, got out of the car and—"

"Excuse me," I interrupted. "But which car was she driving?"

"This one." Culligan pointed to the Cadillac.

Nodding, I waited for him to continue.

"She turned off the headlights and the engine," Culligan said, "and locked the doors of the car. Everything tidy. Meanwhile, the garage door was going down behind her, automatically. Now, the way I figure it"—he turned to face the Ford station wagon—"the assailant was maybe hiding there, behind that wagon."

"Why do you say that?"

He pointed first to a small service door set in the side of the garage facing the house, then pointed to the outline of the body. "She was lying face down," he said, "with her head toward that door, which leads into the house. Normally, she would have gotten out of her car, walked around the front of the car and made for that small door. The light switch is beside that door. She would have turned out the garage lights, which are switched on automatically when the garage door goes up. She would have locked that small door behind her and proceeded through a small covered passageway that leads to the house. I figure that she was just starting in on that routine when her assailant came up behind her and hit her on the head."

"Was that the cause of death?" I asked. "A blow to the head?"

"That's the M.E.'s opinion."

"All right. Go ahead."

"Well, I figure that he hit her, like I said, and then took her purse. Then I figure he went to *that* door, which leads to the garden." He motioned to a second door, set in the back of the garage. "He turned off the lights and went out into the garden." Culligan gestured toward the second door. "Do you want to see?"

"Let's finish in here first." I moved to stand beside the outline of the body. Culligan was right. It could have happened just as he'd reconstructed it. Someone crouched behind the front of the Ford would have been in perfect position to surprise the victim.

"How old was she?" I asked.

"Seventy."

"And you figure someone was waiting for her, to rob her."

Culligan shrugged. "All I'm saying is that it could have happened like that, Frank. I'm not paid to come up with theories."

I ignored the point. At age forty-six, Culligan was still an inspector. Privately, I'd always suspected that he'd rather complain about his status than try for promotion. Culligan was a good detective, but he was a complainer. His wife was a complainer, too. Together, they morosely shook their heads over everything.

For the first time I noticed a separately taped-off section of the concrete floor. The tapes marked a sizable oil stain, over which a powdery, ash-colored substance had been liberally scattered. Someone had spilled oil on the floor, then sprinkled it with absorbent. The oil stain extended along the back wall for perhaps six feet. Anyone crouched behind the Ford would have been forced to step in the oil. Looking closely, I saw that the absorbent mixture had been scattered widely across the concrete. Both the murderer and the victim would have traces of the mixture on their shoes.

"That," Culligan said, "has got to be a break. The oil was spilled yesterday morning."

I stooped to touch the ash-colored material. "Did the victim have any of this on her shoes?" I asked.

"Definitely."

I straightened, nodding. "You're right, it's a break. What about the weapon?"

"It's an iron pipe. It was out in the garden. The lab crew took it."

"Anything else in here?"

"Not really," Culligan answered.

For the first time, Canelli spoke. "There's sure a lot of blood," he said. "He really must've clobbered her."

"He did," Culligan answered shortly. "He *really* clobbered her. Caved in the whole back of her head. Must've hit her a half-dozen times."

"If he used a pipe," Canelli said, "he must've gotten himself all bloody."

"Let's see the garden," I said, gesturing for Culligan to go first. He led the way to the rear service door, pausing to point out jimmy marks on the frame. I glanced at the scratches, then followed Culligan outside. It was a small, European-style garden, beautifully planted. Surrounding the garden was an eight-foot brick wall, painted white. A line of sharpened spikes topped the wall. Between the spikes, I noticed, pieces of broken glass were embedded in the concrete. At the rear of the garden, a small, heavily timbered door gave access to the alley behind. The door was iron-bound, secured with a heavy iron bolt. The Esterbrook-Gaines household was security-conscious.

Noticing me staring at the garden door, Culligan said, "That door was tumbler-locked last night when the murder was committed, but it wasn't bolted. There's jimmy marks on that door, too."

"Do you think the murderer entered that way?"

"Could be," he answered diffidently. "It'd make sense. He jimmies the alley door, enters the garden and jimmies the garage's rear door. He waits inside for her. He hits her, takes her purse, and escapes. He throws the pipe over there—" Culligan pointed to a large laurel bush, identified with the lab's red-and-white evidence tag. "Then he goes out the way he came."

"What about the purse?" Canelli asked.

"Nothing yet," Culligan answered. "But I don't have anyone looking for it. That's not for me to assign." Pointedly, he looked at me. Inspectors were mere drudges, his expression implied.

"How do you know the garden gate wasn't bolted when the murder was committed?" I asked.

"Because the chauffeur came through it after the murder," Culligan answered promptly.

"Jeeze," Canelli said. "A chauffeur. Some class."

"How about the household?" I asked Culligan. "What's the rundown?"

"Well, it's a little tiny bit kinky," Culligan said.

"Kinky?"

"Yeah. This Flora Esterbrook Gaines was seventy years old, like I told you. And her husband, named Rupert Gaines, is only thirty-five." Culligan paused, awaiting our reaction. Canelli, predictably, was dolefully shaking his head, scandalized.

"It seems like she was a wealthy widow until she was sixty-five," Culligan continued. "Then she married this guy Gaines. So they've been married for five years."

"A gigolo."

Again Culligan shrugged. Mere inspectors weren't supposed to judge manners or morals.

"Who else is in the house?"

"There's the chauffeur, like I said." As he spoke, Culligan took out his notebook. Holding the notebook slightly away from his middle-aging eyes, he recited, "Name, Peter Fry. Age forty-nine. He's a combination handyman and chauffeur—does odd jobs and looks after the cars."

"Why wasn't he driving Mrs. Gaines last night?"

"The way I understand it, Mr. and Mrs. Gaines have—had —this habit of going out separately every Tuesday night. They always went out to dinner, then to a movie, or something. Separately, like I said. So Tuesday was the help's night out. Everyone went his own way, you might say."

"Where'd Peter Fry go?"

Culligan's sallow, humorless face drew down into lines of dry disdain. "Fry was out drinking. The way I get it, from the maid, Fry is a lush. What happens, apparently, is that he goes out drinking three nights a week, without fail. Tuesdays, Thursdays, Saturdays. A real hard-core drinker, in other words. So last night, as usual, he was out drinking at a neighborhood bar. He left the bar just before twelve, he says, and came home. And that's how I know when the garden door was bolted—the door leading to the alley."

"How's that?"

"Fry always comes home down the alley," Culligan answered. "He always comes in through that door. He opens the door with his key, then closes it behind him and shoots the bolt. It's one of those household routines. The alley door, see, is Fry's responsibility. Every night, he bolts it. When he's home, he bolts it at dark. When he goes out, he bolts it when he comes in. Without fail."

"And once that door's bolted," Canelli offered, "the place is buttoned up tight."

As Culligan nodded, I led the way to the garden door. After verifying that the door had been dusted for prints, I stepped out into the narrow alley. "Which way did Fry come from?" I asked.

"That way." Culligan pointed toward the east. "And he says that when he was entering the alley from that direction he thought—repeat, thought—he saw someone coming out of this door. Or, at least, someone was coming out of *some* door along here. A so-called shadowy figure, according to Fry."

"Do you believe him?"

Culligan spread his bony hands. "Who knows? You can talk to him, see what you think. But the time sequence would be about right."

"Which way did this shadowy figure go?"

Culligan pointed to the west end of the alley. "He went down there, Fry says."

"Was Fry drunk at the time?"

"Who knows? Probably."

"Hey, Lieutenant," Canelli said. "Want me to take a look down there?" He pointed in the direction the murderer could have gone. "Maybe I can find something. Her purse, maybe."

I nodded. "Good idea. Check the ashcans before they're picked up. I'll get a couple of patrolmen to help you."

"Right." Amiably, hands in his pockets, Canelli strolled off. No other detective on my squad would have volunteered so cheerfully to search through trash.

Turning back to the Gaines garden, I asked, "Who else is in the household?"

Culligan flipped the neatly written pages of his notebook. "The maid," he answered. "Charlotte Young."

"What's her story?"

"Her story is that she's one of these black militants. Age, twenty-three. About the first thing she told me was that she's only working as a maid so that she can go to law school, if you can believe that."

"Why wouldn't I believe it?"

Not replying, Culligan glowered down at his notes. Like most policemen, he was at war with the blacks.

"What's her story?" I pressed.

"Her story is that she was the only one home last night. Mr. and Mrs. Gaines went out for dinner and the evening, like I said. Peter Fry went out about nine P.M. Charlotte Young stayed home, studying. She's the one that made the call. The call came in at twelve twenty-two A.M., according to Dispatch."

"She discovered the body?" We were walking through the garden toward the house. As we passed the red-and-white-tagged laurel bush, I glanced at a smear of blood on the leaves.

Culligan nodded. "She discovered the body. Charlotte Young's room is in the back of the house on the second floor. She's closest to the garage, and she can hear the garage door whenever it goes up and down, apparently. She was awake when the victim came home, a little after midnight. She heard the garage door go up, then down, as usual. Then nothing. She thought Mrs. Gaines was still in the garage because she hadn't heard the back door open. So, to check, Charlotte Young looked down at the garage, expecting to see the lights still on inside. When she saw that the garage was dark, she got suspicious."

"How long did all this take?"

Culligan shrugged. "Not more than a few minutes if her story's right. I've got a couple of patrolmen checking to see if any of the neighbors can verify what time Mrs. Gaines came home."

"What happened next?"

"Charlotte Young decided to go downstairs and investigate. But, while she was getting into her bathrobe, she heard something else—some other sound. She thought it was the garden door, but she's not completely sure because she was in her closet—getting into her bathrobe, like I said. So then, about a minute later, she went to the window again. And she saw Peter Fry coming in."

"What'd he do? Anything unusual?"

He shook his head. "Nothing. He just staggered into the garden, bolted the door and then staggered toward the house."

"If her story is right," I said thoughtfully, "the murderer was letting himself out the alley door while she was getting into her robe."

"Right."

"And, also, her story tends to confirm Fry's. So far, it all fits."

"I know."

"What next?"

"Well, next, she apparently waited for Fry to come into the house and go to the bathroom and enter his own bedroom. Fry's room is also at the back of the house. But it's three doors down from Charlotte's, on the opposite side of the house. The east side."

"Away from the garage, you mean."

"Yeah."

I frowned. "Did Charlotte say why she waited for Fry to go into his own room? I mean, if she were worried about Mrs. Gaines, I'd think she'd want to have Fry with her, for support."

Culligan grimaced. "When you meet Charlotte, you'll see that she doesn't need support. From anyone."

When I didn't comment, Culligan continued, "Charlotte went down to the kitchen and entered the back hallway—without turning on the lights. She found the back door locked. She entered the covered passageway leading to the garage. The side access door to the garage was also locked. She—"

"Did Charlotte have a key with her?"

"I'm not sure." He hesitated, eyeing me with faint resentment. Culligan didn't like to be cross-questioned. "Anyhow," he continued brusquely, "she entered the garage. Immediately, she says, she knew there was something wrong—because of the smell."

"Did she turn on the lights?"

"No. There was enough light coming through the garage doors, she claims, to see the body. I checked it last night. She could've seen it, all right, without switching on the lights."

"So then she called us."

"Right. She used the kitchen phone. The call came in to Dispatch at twenty-two minutes after midnight, like I said. So, if Charlotte's story is right, there was maybe ten or fifteen minutes elapsed between the time Mrs. Gaines entered the garage and the time Charlotte discovered her body."

"It sounds right," I mused. "So far, it sounds right."

Noncommittally, Culligan looked away. As he'd said, he preferred not to theorize.

"So what we've got," I said thoughtfully, gazing around the beautifully kept grounds, "is apparently a mugger who forced his way into the garden, forced his way into the garage and hid himself, waiting for Mrs. Gaines to come home. We've got her coming home at about midnight. We've got the assailant hitting her on the head and taking her purse, apparently. Then we've got the assailant escaping the same way he came, at maybe ten minutes after midnight. Fry, possibly, saw the murderer escaping." Absently, I snapped a bloom from a towering fuchsia bush. "On the surface," I said, "it seems pretty pat. Is that the way it seems to you?"

Culligan was frowning, thoughtfully chewing at his thin lips. Finally he said cryptically, "Like you say, it's pretty pat —on the surface. Beneath the surface, I'm not so sure. This Rupert Gaines—the husband—he sure doesn't seem very broken up, to me."

"Maybe he's just being a realist. After all, he stands to inherit some money, probably."

"Yeah," Culligan said. "That's Charlotte Young's theory."

I looked at him. "Has Charlotte Young got a theory?"

"I think so."

"Then I'll start with her."

Five

I watched Charlotte Young cross her small room and turn to face me. She was dressed in a gleaming white nylon maid's uniform. Beside her on the wall, a huge picture of Che Guevara glowered at me. The girl was glowering, too.

"I didn't get much sleep last night," she said. "And I've got lots of work to do. Especially now." She stood with her arms folded, back straight, legs spread at a wide, militant angle.

"There're just a few more questions, Miss Young."

She didn't reply. Her gaze was steady, street-corner-cool. She was a stocky, muscular girl. Beneath the short white skirt her thighs were thickly muscled. Above the folded arms her breasts swelled in a full, defiant curve. She wore her hair natural, clipped close to her scalp. She carried her head with a high, hostile arrogance. Her skin was a deep, velvet black, a mark of pride in the Negro community. Her features were classic Negroid—wide jaw, full lips, a thick Bantu nose. Her eyes were quick and calm.

"What questions are those?" she asked.

"I understand," I began, "that you're going to law school. Is that right?"

"That's right." She spoke aggressively, as if she dared me to deny it.

"When you pass the bar, you'll be an officer of the court."

Waiting for the hook, she made no reply.

"Has it occurred to you that Mrs. Gaines might not have been killed for the money in her purse, Miss Young?"

For a moment she didn't reply. Then, slowly, she nodded. "It occurred to me, yes."

"A mugger wouldn't've known Mrs. Gaines's schedule. He couldn't've known that she was out alone last night. A mugger works on the street, taking what comes along."

Her lip curled. "You don't have to tell me about muggers. I grew up in Hunter's Point, Lieutenant. The jungle."

"We just heard from our police lab that the killer apparently wore rubber gloves—surgical gloves," I continued. "That doesn't sound much like a mugger, either."

Still with her arms folded, she sank down on the arm of the room's only easy chair. "So what's the point, Lieutenant? Are you saying that I killed Mrs. Gaines? Is that it?"

"No, that's not it," I answered. "That's not it at all. I'm asking whether you know of anyone who might've killed her, or hired someone to do the job."

Now her lips were curving into a small, sardonic smile. "I'd be pretty stupid, wouldn't I, to answer a question like that?"

"Why?"

"You talk about the law. There's libel, you know."

I shook my head. "Not when you're talking to a police officer. Not when you're answering a direct request for information. It's just the opposite, in fact. Technically, if you refuse to answer, you're obstructing justice."

The sardonic smile widened. "Big deal."

I decided to wait, watching her make up her mind. I could guess at her problem. In Hunter's Point, you didn't talk to the police. But I was giving her a chance to take a free crack at whitey. Plainly, she was tempted.

"What about her husband?" I pressed. "Rupert Gaines?"

"What *about* him?" It was a contemptuous question.

"Could he have killed her?"

She snorted. "Have you talked to Mr. Gaines yet?"

"No."

"Well, when you *do* talk to him, you'll see that he isn't exactly a homicidal type, Lieutenant."

"What type is he, then?"

"He's more of a limp-wrist, chicken-shit type. Very unheavy."

"He's only thirty-five, I understand. And his wife was seventy."

"That's right, Lieutenant. I guess that tells you something right there, doesn't it?"

I smiled. "I guess it does. How long have you been working for the Gaineses?"

"Almost two years."

"How long have they been married?"

"Five years. Flora's husband, the millionaire, died when she was sixty. When she was sixty-five, she decided to go on a world cruise. Rupert was working at her travel agency. So, naturally, they ended up taking the trip together, as man and wife. Rupert might be a little limp-wristed, but he's not stupid. Like, he's got a travel agency of his own now. With two or three branch offices, at the last count."

"Do you know anything about the rest of Mrs. Gaines's family?"

"As a matter of fact, I do. I'm a listener, Lieutenant. It's surprising how much you learn if you listen."

I nodded. "I agree. So talk."

"Well, there's her son, Jonathan Esterbrook. And her daughter, Grace Esterbrook Carstairs. They're both in their forties. Jonathan is a middle-aged fag. Grace is a middle-aged social climber."

I suppressed a smile. "When you start talking, you talk pretty good." I entered the names in my notebook. "Do Jonathan Esterbrook and Grace Carstairs live in the city?"

"Jonathan lives on Telegraph Hill, naturally. And, naturally, Grace lives in Pacific Heights."

"Are they both well-off? Financially, I mean."

She shrugged. "They sure *look* well-off."

"Did they get along well with Mrs. Gaines?"

"As far as I know, they did. Of course, nobody exactly treated me like a member of the family, you know. I'm just telling you how things looked to me."

"What about Peter Fry, the chauffeur?"

"What *about* him?"

"Could he have murdered Mrs. Gaines, would you say?"

"All he cares about is drinking," she answered decisively. "But he's cool. He's got it all worked out. He goes from drink to drink, bottle to bottle. He's never drunk on the job, though. I'll give him that."

"You haven't answered my question."

"Could he have *killed* her, you mean?" Her retort touched a high, derisive note, echoing the aw-shucks hoot of the ghetto. "I just *told* you. All Peter cares about is drinking. He looks into that bottle, he sees it all. Everything. Like I say, he's cool."

I glanced at my watch, then rose to my feet. "I have just one more question, Miss Young."

"What's that?"

"I'd like to know what kind of a person Mrs. Gaines was —how she struck you. Was she careless about her personal safety, for instance—or cautious?"

"She was a cagey old crow," came the prompt answer. "Nobody put much over on her. She wasn't any great intellect. But she had a kind of low cunning, I guess you'd say. Like, I always figured she was pretty smart, keeping the ring in Rupert's nose, without letting it pinch too much."

"How do you mean?"

"Well, for instance, she was smart enough to give him toys without him asking. To preserve his so-called masculine pride."

"Toys?"

"His travel agency. She set it up for him. Which was pretty smart, see, because if the agency made money, she didn't have to put Rupert on an allowance. And if it lost money, then she could take a tax loss." Charlotte Young tapped her forehead. "It's like I say, she was cagey."

"And did the agency make money?"

She smiled. "It never would've made much money with just Rupert running it. Which, of course, was the way Flora figured. But what she *didn't* figure on was a filly named Susan Platt."

"Who's Susan Platt?"

"Susan Platt is Rupert's partner. And it turns out that Susan's a winner. She took that little old travel agency and turned it into a moneymaker. All in the last year or two."

"How did Mrs. Gaines like that?" I asked thoughtfully.

She shrugged, pushed herself away from the arm of the chair and came toward me. Her arms were still folded, boldly displaying her breasts. "I guess she had mixed feelings, like they say. She probably liked the part about how she was making money on her investment, instead of losing it. But she probably didn't like how that ring was getting a little loose in hubby's nose."

I thanked her for her trouble and left her where I found her—beside her Che Guevara poster. I descended the back stairway, entering the kitchen by the servants' door. We'd taken over the Gaines kitchen for an improvised command post. As I entered I saw Canelli sitting on a high stool. Looking at his complacent expression, I knew that he'd discovered something. The Canelli luck was holding.

He pointed to a large clear-plastic evidence bag lying on the counter beside him. Inside the bag was an alligator purse and a red leather wallet.

"I just happened to see it lying in a rose bush," Canelli said. "It was down by the end of the alley. The west end. The suspect tossed it over a fence, I guess."

"So he did run toward the west." I lifted the evidence bag to get a better look inside. The wallet was empty. "What about credit cards?" I asked.

"They're there. A lot of them, anyhow."

"Has Culligan come back yet?"

"No, sir."

"When he comes back," I said, "I think he should get started looking into Mrs. Gaines's background. Tell him to get her safe-deposit box sealed if he hasn't done it already. Then he should detail someone to get a court order to look at her will. He can use Sigler, if he wants. Tell Culligan to give it the whole treatment. Everything. I'm going to talk to Mr. Gaines and to Peter Fry. Then I'm going to see whether I can talk to the victim's son and daughter. Meanwhile, I want you to call the General Works Detail and ask them to do a little listening for us. Find out if there's any rumble about a mugger being involved in this. Also, have General Works check out anyone with an M.O. that could fit."

"Yes, sir." Canelli was climbing down from his stool, frowning heavily as he committed my orders to memory.

"Where's Mr. Gaines, do you know?"

"I think he's in the living room, Lieutenant. He was going to go out to the funeral parlor, but I told him—asked him—to stick around. He didn't seem too happy about it."

Dressed in an elegantly cut dark suit, Rupert Gaines was sitting on a brocaded silk French Provincial armchair. He sat with legs crossed, one elbow propped on a slim thigh, chin resting in a cupped palm. With his dark, longish hair and his thin, pale face, he could have been a Victorian poet, brooding in some distant drawing room.

"Mr. Gaines?"

He slowly turned his head, allowing his forearm to fall languidly down along his thigh. "Are you Lieutenant Hastings?" His voice was low and melodic, a perfect complement to his poet's moody good looks.

"Yes. I wonder if I could talk to you for a few minutes? I realize it's a bad time. But I've got to get a few things settled."

"Why not," he sighed, gesturing me to a facing chair. As I sat down, I glanced through a huge picture window at a spectacular sweep of the ocean.

"Have you found him?" Gaines asked.

"The murderer, you mean?"

He slowly, dramatically nodded.

"No, we haven't," I answered.

"Do you have any clues?"

"Not really. Nothing conclusive. But I wouldn't worry about it, Mr. Gaines. Homicide investigations take a while. We can't afford to make mistakes."

He frowned, studying me with dark eyes that seemed curiously opaque, utterly expressionless. "But you're sure, at least, that it's a professional criminal," he said dully.

I deliberately shook my head. "At this point, Mr. Gaines, we aren't sure of anything. That's why I need your help."

He nodded wearily. "All right. Whatever I can do."

"Good." I leaned toward him, getting down to business. "First, I'd like to know if there's anyone—anyone at all—who you think might have wanted to harm your wife. Had she ever been threatened? Did she have any enemies?"

"But—" He licked at his lips. "But her purse was stolen. She was—was robbed by a stranger. A—a complete stranger. How would I know anything about that?"

"For the moment, let's forget about robbery, Mr. Gaines. Of course, it's a possibility. A probability, in fact. But there are other possibilities, too. And it's my job to look into everything. Do you understand?"

"Are—are you asking me to give you the name of someone who could have killed her? Is that what you're asking?"

"That's what I'm asking, Mr. Gaines."

"But I—I can't. There's no one. No one at all."

Covertly watching him, I allowed a long moment of silence to pass. If he was acting out the part of the bereaved husband, I decided, he was doing a credible job.

"You're sure there's no one? Absolutely sure?"

He nodded.

"Then let me ask you this, Mr. Gaines—" I paused, pitching my voice to a neutral, offhand note. "Let me ask you about her heirs. Who would've profited by her death?"

Plainly, the question startled him. For the first time since I'd entered the room, his empty, opaque eyes came into sharp focus. Instantly, his manner changed. "*What?*" It was an outraged monosyllable, spoken in a high, shocked falsetto. "*What?*"

"I'm asking you who—"

"Are you accusing me? *Me?*"

"Mr. Gaines, I'm just trying to find out, as a matter of simple fact, who—"

"That other one. Inspector Culligan. He—he's got my—my *clothes.* When I asked him why he wanted them—when I *insisted* on knowing, he admitted that he wanted to see if there was blood on them. *Blood.*" His voice was rising, outraged.

"But you see, Mr. Gaines, that's really for your own protection, when you think about it. We try to eliminate—"

"My protection? From what, may I ask?"

I drew a long, deep breath, hopefully to calm him. I didn't want him excited, off the deep end. "As you probably know, Mr. Gaines, your wife was murdered in such a way that the murderer must've gotten blood on his clothes. Now, the plain fact is that, when a wife is murdered, it's routine for us to check out her husband. We've *got* to do it. We've got to—"

"I think I should get a lawyer. I don't have to answer these questions. You—you're supposed to give me my constitutional rights."

"You're right," I answered quietly. "You *don't* have to answer. But you're wrong when you say that I'm supposed to give you your rights. That's only necessary, according to the law, when an officer is questioning a suspect. And you're not a suspect. I'm merely asking you for information."

"Why're you testing my clothes for blood if I'm not a suspect?" Suddenly he rose, crossing to an ornate onyx fireplace. He rested one elbow on the mantelpiece, indignantly posing for me. Waywardly, I wondered how much time he spent posed like that.

"Would it make you feel better," I asked slowly, "if I gave you your constitutional rights?"

He blinked at the question. For a moment we stared silently at each other. Then he shrugged uncertainly. Having scored a minor point, I decided to shift my ground. "Do you know what your wife intended to do last night, Mr. Gaines?"

"Certainly. She was going to have dinner at Fisherman's Wharf. Alioto's, I think. Then she was going to a movie."

"Do you happen to know how much money she was carrying?"

He shrugged. "Not much, probably. Flora was very careful about money. She used credit cards."

"Do you know which movie she saw?"

"As a matter of fact, I do. She was going to the Clay. They were showing two old Humphrey Bogart pictures. My wife—" Suddenly he gulped, biting his lip. "My wife was a Bogart fan. I am, too."

"And what about you, Mr. Gaines? What did you do last night?"

For a moment he didn't reply. I saw his chest heave, as if he were struggling to stifle a sob. Was it genuine emotion—or skillful deception? I watched him closely as he shook his head in a slow, baffled arc, avoiding my eyes. Finally, speaking in a low, subdued voice, he said, "I had dinner with my business partner. Her name is Susan Platt. She—she had some problems to talk over with me. Business problems. We ate at Monroe's. Then I took her home. She gave me a brandy, and I left a little before eleven. I've *told* all this to Inspector Culligan."

"What'd you do then? After you left Susan Platt's house?"

"I had a few drinks on Union Street. At the Cooperage. Susan lives near Union. I went to the Cooperage so I wouldn't have to repark my car. Then I went to a couple of other bars. I—I didn't get home until quarter of one. And by then, of course . . ." Shoulders sagging, he turned dispiritedly away from the onyx fireplace. Stumbling slightly, face averted, he moved to stand before the picture window.

If it was an act, I decided to go along with it. "Thank you, Mr. Gaines," I said sotto voce. "I won't bother you any longer. If you have something you'd like to do—some arrangements to make, please go ahead. We won't be needing you for a while now."

When he nodded silently, I left the room.

Six

I found Peter Fry, the chauffeur, in a small utility room behind the garage. The room was crowded with lawn furniture and gardening tools, fertilizer sacks and flower pots. One wall of shelves was lined with automotive accessories: cans of oil, wrenches, fan belts and polishing equipment. The room was dim, lit only by the uncertain light from two small windows, one of them overgrown with vines. Wondering whether Culligan had established a chain of evidence to account for the spilled oil and ash-colored absorbent compound on the garage floor, I stepped close to the collection of automotive cans and cartons.

"It's called Kleen-Eeze, Lieutenant. And Detective Culligan's already got it."

I turned to face Fry. He was sitting on a low workbench, legs idly dangling. He was a man in his late forties, thin, medium height. His face was prematurely lined, his watery blue eyes permanently defeated. His sparse, ginger-colored hair was uncombed. Ginger eyebrows grew in tufts above the deep-set eyes, as if the eyebrows had been pasted on the face as a joke. He wore stained, wrinkled trousers and an old, baggy red sweater. He sat with his hands braced wide at his sides, fingers spread. The fingers scratched incessantly at the bench's wooden top, responding to some small, secret spasm of anxiety. Moving constantly around the room, his restless loser's eyes were never still, never at ease. He could only meet my eye for brief moments before his gaze fled aside. Fry's appearance matched Culligan's description of him—a lush, gone to seed. Only Fry's shoes were well-kept, burnished to a rich cordovan sheen.

Seeing my eyes on his shoes, Fry laughed softly. "I was always taught," he said, "that you could tell a gentleman by his boots. I learned that in military school, many years ago. Did Detective Culligan tell you that I went to military school? Did he tell you that I'm a—" He burped. "That I'm an ex-officer and an ex-gentleman?"

As he spoke, I moved closer—close enough to catch the strong odor of liquor. Watching me, he nodded owlishly.

"That's right, Lieutenant. I'm drunk. As one officer to another, there's no point in denying it. I'm in deep, alcoholic mourning for my dead employer. I'm also in mourning for myself. Mostly, I suppose, for myself. You see, I first entered Mrs. Esterbrook's service when I was only forty-one years old. That was eight years ago, Lieutenant. Eight long, long years ago." He broke off, dolefully shaking his head. Then, abruptly, he asked, "How old are you?"

Surprised, I hesitated before answering, "Forty-three."

"Hmm—" He cocked his head to one side, studying me with exaggerated care, his eyes half-closed. "You have," he said, "the appearance of a man who's capable of a certain sympathy. You're tough, I'm sure. Very, very tough. But you're probably protecting a certain softness within, just like the rest of us. It's an attribute that someone like myself—a flawed vessel, as they say—can sense quite readily. And, yes—" He ponderously nodded. "Yes, I can see that you have some perception of what makes lesser men tick."

As he said it, I secretly winced. For two years after my marriage broke up—for a year after I joined the force—I'd been a solitary drinker. I'd only stopped drinking when Captain Kreiger, then a homicide lieutenant and an old army friend, had found me drunk in my apartment one night, off duty. The cold, quiet lash of Kreiger's voice and the contempt in his eyes had been the shock I'd needed. The next day I knocked on the door of Kreiger's office and told him that I'd thrown away the liquor. Entering that office had taken more strength than I knew I possessed.

"And so now," Fry was saying, "you're here to administer some sort of *coup de grâce*. Is that it? Detective Culligan, I'm sure, has made his report. He's told you that I was abroad at the time of the murder. Right?"

"My information is that you may have seen the murderer leaving the premises last night."

"Yes," he answered, mock gravely, "I suppose that's true. As I told Detective Culligan, I saw a slim, shadowy figure dressed in a topcoat and a felt hat. He was acting very suspiciously—very furtively. In fact, he was acting just like he'd murdered somebody. Except that I don't think Detective Culligan believes me. I'm afraid he thinks that I'm trying to throw him off the scent. Is that what you think, too, Lieutenant?"

I decided not to reply. If he was willing to continue his alcoholic's maudlin monologue, I was willing to listen.

"Of course," Fry was saying, "I suppose there's the question of why I would have killed her. I'm sure Detective Culligan thinks I murdered her for the money. My inheritance. Is that what you think, Lieutenant?"

"Outside of people getting drunk on Saturday night and shooting each other for no reason," I answered quietly, "money is the most common motive for murder."

"Exactly." He raised a professional forefinger, winking at me. "Precisely. Except that, in my case, I've already discovered the evil that money can do. Or, to be more exact, I've discovered the evil that an *inheritance* can do. You see, my inheritance set me on the downward path, no question. I was thirty-two at the time, and I had a promising career in front of me, selling real estate. Of course, I had a shattered career behind me, too. But that's another story." He paused, eyeing me with a playfully boozy camaraderie. "Unless, of course, you'd like to hear the complete, uncensored story of my life. Would you?"

"Sure."

"Ah, good." He drew himself up on the workbench, burlesquing a sober-sided recitation. "Actually, you already know the first part—military school, where I was sent because I was in the way at home. Whereupon, at age eighteen, I was commissioned in the Signal Corps, and sent away to fight Hitler —probably because I was in someone's way in America. However, I emerged from the war a captain. So, naturally, I decided to become a career army officer. I even married the daughter of my commanding officer, which is considered very good technique in the peacetime army. But my wife developed an unfortunate habit of sleeping with other men—officers, of course. Never enlisted men. So I began to drink. And, finally, I became an embarrassment to myself and others, as the saying goes. My commanding officer—not my wife's father —suggested that I resign my commission. I did. I was thirty-one years old at the time, and I became a real-estate salesman. I sold real estate down in Los Angeles, where it's almost impossible to go broke selling real estate. Except that—" He paused for breath. Momentarily the drunken rush of his story faltered, plainly the prey of a painful rush of memory. But, almost instantly, he recovered his clown's comic touch.

Coughing to cover the lapse, he continued, "Except that I didn't quit drinking while I was selling real estate. Maybe, if my father hadn't died, I *would* have quit. Drinking, I mean. I thought about it. But then my father died, and I got my inheritance. It would have been foolish, of course, to quit drinking, with all that money to spend. So, the next thing I knew, it was ten years later. All the money was gone, but I was still drinking. Except that, by that time, I was drinking muscatel. I was in San Francisco, on skid row. I never quite knew how I got to San Francisco, except that I'd always liked it here. But, after years of drinking Scotch, both as an officer and a gentleman and also as a young man with means, the muscatel had a—" Suddenly he burped, then rotated his head in loose, amiable apology. "The muscatel had a very—sobering effect, if you catch my meaning. I realized that if I didn't take countermeasures, as they say in the army, before my good blue suit got frayed, I'd be outflanked. So I got a haircut and got the blue suit pressed. And, of course—" He stared down at his gleaming cordovan shoes. "Of course, I shined my shoes. Then I went to the employment office. Flora, as it happened, was looking for a driver and handyman. I was looking for a job. So—*voilà*—we found each other." He waved his hand in the air, doing a bad imitation of a continental gentleman.

"And now you're in her will."

Eyes closed, he solemnly nodded.

"For how much money, do you know?"

"Several thousand, so she said. Which, of course, could mean anything." He was still staring down at his shoes, slowly swinging back and forth beneath the workbench. I heard him sigh. His boozy ebullience was fading.

"Do you know who else is in her will?"

He shrugged. "She didn't confide in me to that extent. She told me that I'd get several thousand. For past services rendered."

I watched him a moment, then said quietly, "Were some of the services rendered in bed?"

For a long, head-down moment he didn't reply. Then, slowly, he raised his eyes. Despair was deeply etched into every line of his ravaged face. Slowly he shrugged. "We do what we have to do, Lieutenant. And anything's better than muscatel."

"I can see," I said slowly, "that you wouldn't have wanted her to die. You need your job."

"Yes," he answered. "Yes, I need the job. I don't have much luck with inheritances." He tried to smile. "I can't afford them."

"Others, though, might have wanted her to die. Have you thought about it?"

"Yes," he answered heavily. "Yes, I've thought about it."

"Then give me a name."

"A name?"

I nodded. "Who would have wanted her dead, Fry? Someone knew her habits, planned her murder. Who was it?"

"I—" He began to shake his head, hopelessly. "I don't know."

"Did Charlotte Young inherit anything?"

"I don't think so."

"Then there was you, her husband, her daughter and her son. You all inherited. Was there anyone else?"

"No one, probably. Except—" He hesitated, blinking at a sudden thought.

42

"Except who?"

"Except her daughter's husband. Charles Carstairs. He wouldn't inherit. But he'd profit."

"Is that the name you're giving me?"

"I don't know what to—" At that instant, a knock sounded. The door was just behind me. I turned impatiently, jerking the door open. I was facing Canelli.

"I'm sorry to bother you, Lieutenant," he said, glancing anxiously past me toward Fry.

"What is it, Canelli?" I stepped quickly out into the garden, pulling the door closed behind me.

"Charles Carstairs just came. He's Mrs. Gaines's son-in-law," Canelli said softly. "He wants to see the person in charge. I thought I should tell you."

"What's his problem?"

"I'm not really sure. Except that he's the kind who's used to raising stinks, I'd say. Well-mannered stinks. The big-shot type."

I considered a moment, then lowered my voice. "All right, I'll talk to him. Where is he?"

"In the living room."

Ordering Canelli to question Fry concerning his precise movements the night before, I entered the Gaines house through the back entrance, retracing the route I'd taken earlier. I found a tall, middle-aged man standing haughtily in the exact center of the elaborately furnished living room. He was dressed in fifty-dollar shoes and a two-hundred-dollar topcoat. His iron-gray hair was stockbroker-mod. The "V" of his expensive topcoat revealed an old school tie. He was the perfect picture of affluent success.

"Are you Lieutenant Hastings?" Before I could reply, he continued, "I'm Charles Carstairs. My wife is Grace Esterbrook Carstairs. Does the name mean anything to you, Lieutenant?"

"It does."

"Good." He nodded urbanely, then advanced on me with a slow, confident step. His conservative horn-rimmed glasses and military-style mustache were perfect complements to the old school tie. Even the face, lean and aristocratic, seemed somehow modeled on the Brooks Brothers style, as if nature had followed the ads. "Then you're the person I want to talk to," he said.

"Fine." I gestured to a nearby sofa. "Shall we sit down?"

"I'm afraid I don't have time, Lieutenant. Actually, all I wanted to say was that, representing the family, I'd like to make sure that you'll, ah, refrain from intruding until after my mother-in-law's funeral."

"Intruding?"

"Yes. My wife, as you can imagine, is terribly upset. Jonathan, my mother-in-law's son, is also upset—in his own way. Actually, I don't know whether you'd intended to question them. Or, for that matter, me. But I thought I should tell you that we'd, ah, very much appreciate it if you'd wait a decent interval. At the right time, of course, we'd be glad to answer your questions."

I decided to pretend puzzlement. Frowning, I asked, "You're the spokesman for the family?"

"Yes. I'm making the funeral arrangements."

"But only blood relatives can make funeral arrangements, Mr. Carstairs. That's the law. And, in fact, I understood that Mr. Gaines was making the arrangements."

Plainly annoyed, he nodded impatiently. "I've come to talk to Gaines. But I wanted to talk to you first. You see, it's a matter of—"

"You don't have to bother, Carstairs." It was Gaines's voice, behind me. Turning, I stepped back, making room for him to enter. "The arrangements are already made," he said. "In fact, I'm just going to take Flora's dress to the funeral parlor."

For a moment Carstairs was silent, making an obvious effort at self control. Finally, speaking slowly and distinctly, he said, "Grace will be over soon, Gaines. She'll get her mother's things."

"You heard what the lieutenant said. Legally, I'm the one responsible."

The two men were facing each other in the middle of the room. In some respects they were similar. Both were finely drawn types, too civilized to say what they were really think-

44

ing. But, plainly, they didn't like each other. I withdrew another cautious step. Listening, I could learn a lot.

Carstairs drew a deep, determined breath. "You might be the one who's legally responsible, Gaines. You married her. But, morally, you don't even have a right to attend the funeral, much less make the arrangements."

Gaines's lip curled. He reminded me of a spoiled, unpleasant child, about to hurl an insult from a safe distance before ducking around a corner. "You're in my house, Carstairs," he said. "Why don't you leave?"

"Because it isn't your house. Half this house belongs to Grace. The other half belongs to Jonathan. You'll get a few thousand dollars for your trouble. Just like the chauffeur."

Suddenly Gaines's pale, poet's face purpled. Clenching his fists, he took a quick, furious step toward his antagonist. Speaking in a low, choked voice, he said, "You're wrong, Carstairs. Just like you're wrong about everything else you do."

"Oh?" Carstairs affected a dry, eyebrow-raised sneer. But his voice shook as he said, "And you're a success. Is that it?"

"I've got a going business that's making money. Which is more than you've ever had. And I've got a house. *This* house. It's half mine, and you goddamn well know it. Half mine, and a quarter your wife's. And a quarter Jonathan's. Just like the rest of Flora's property. You see, Carstairs, Flora changed her will. You didn't know it. *Nobody* knew it but Flora and me and her lawyer."

While Gaines's face was flushed with fury, Carstairs had gone pale. "If I were you, Gaines, I'd check with the lawyer, Harold Rodgers. I think you'll find that Flora never signed that new will. She might have told Rodgers, in your presence, that she was thinking of making changes. But that's not the will she signed. The valid will is in her safe-deposit box." Carstairs managed a twitching, sardonic smile. "I'm afraid Flora was just dangling a carrot. Sorry."

For a moment Gaines's mouth worked soundlessly. Finally: "What'd you do, have her killed before she could sign the new will? Is that what happened?"

Carstairs' glance flicked aside, toward me. Momentarily he struggled for control before he said slowly, "That's libelous,

Gaines. This time, you've really screwed yourself. You've libeled me in front of a police officer."

"Not if it's the truth, I haven't libeled you," Gaines retorted furiously.

"If anyone had her killed, it was probably you. You've just admitted that you thought she'd changed her will—that half of everything was yours. So why should you wait?"

Gaines's forefinger trembled as he pointed toward the hallway. "Get out of here, Carstairs. Get out, and stay out. Tell your wife and her fag brother that I'll see them at the funeral." As he said it, Gaines advanced again on Carstairs, raising a threatening hand, half hysterically. His voice had slipped to a higher note, almost a falsetto.

Carstairs looked down at Gaines's raised hand, now clenched into a fist. Slowly, deliberately, Carstairs' mouth twisted into a smile. "If you hit me, I won't have to bother about libel. I'll have you jailed for assault."

"And if you don't get out of here, I'll have you jailed for trespassing." Gaines's voice was still cracking ineffectually.

Carstairs nodded sardonically, then shook his head in a slow, elaborately patronizing arc. "If you'll just check with Flora's lawyer, Gaines, you'll discover which one of us is trespassing." Carstairs glanced at me, nodded again, and strode quickly to the entry hall. In the archway he turned, saying to me, "You'll have to excuse him, Lieutenant." He gestured negligently toward Gaines, who was standing with back furiously arched, legs spread wide, face still purpled. "No class," Carstairs said, mock regretfully. "No class at all."

Seven

I slammed the car door and settled back in the seat, closing my eyes. I was feeling the effects of the sleep I'd lost the night before.

"Jonathan Esterbrook lives in the four-hundred block of Greenwich Street," I told Canelli. "You can go out California to Grant Avenue, then turn to the—"

"Inspectors Eleven." It was the radio. Sighing, I reached for the microphone.

"Lieutenant Friedman wants you to call him." I recognized Cunningham's voice in Communications.

I acknowledged the message and pointed to a call box on the next corner. Nodding, Canelli parked at a convenient fire hydrant. Moments later I was talking to Friedman.

"How's it going?" he asked.

"I think the butler did it."

"That's real class. A beautiful touch."

"Thanks."

"Can you be down here at four-thirty?" he asked.

"Sure. What's up?"

"Rankin, from the city attorney's office, wants to see you."

For a moment I didn't reply. Rankin was handling the city's defense against the James Biggs damage suit.

"Is this Rankin's idea, or yours?" I asked finally.

"Fifty-fifty," Friedman grunted.

I decided to wait for him to finish.

"What happened," Friedman said finally, "is that I succeeded in breaking down Sonny Blake. Which didn't take too much doing, since Sonny isn't really very bright. And it seems that, sure enough, it was probably James Biggs that hired him to tail you. So I thought that—"

"And Ann, too," I interrupted. "The son of a bitch is tailing Ann."

I heard Friedman sigh. "That's the reason I decided to call Rankin. I may as well tell you."

"Because Biggs is harassing Ann?"

"No. Because I knew you'd get hot. Which you're doing. So I thought we'd better talk about it. With Rankin."

"What's there to talk about? If we can nail Biggs for conspiracy to harass a police officer, we can jail him. Screw his damage suit."

"That's true," Friedman said, elaborately patient. "However, if we *don't* nail him, then he has a free shot at us. Or, more to the point, you. And I don't think Rankin and company would like that. If Biggs gets a free shot at you, he also gets a free shot at the city and county of San Francisco. Anyhow, come back at four-thirty. I'll fill you in. We can—"

"*Wait* a minute. Are you telling me that Sonny Blake has absolutely confessed that James Biggs hired him to—"

"No. That's the point. That's *not* what I'm telling you. If you remember, I said that Biggs *probably* hired him. What actually happened, Blake was hired anonymously—by someone answering Biggs's description. So, before we could get anywhere, we'd have to have Sonny Blake identify Biggs. It would have to be done officially, in a line-up. Right?"

"Listen, Pete, you know there's a hundred ways to—"

"For it to be airtight, it would have to be done in a line-up. And if Blake doesn't make an identification, then we're up the creek. We'd be handing Bigg's lawyers a beautiful case of police harassment. And, besides all that, it's conceivable, you know, that this whole exercise could be a mousetrap."

"What'd you mean, a mousetrap?"

"I mean that Biggs might be harassing us so that we'll harass him. Which, I'm sure, his lawyers would love, like I said. Did you ever think of that?"

"You're giving Biggs a lot of credit."

"You don't know this character," Friedman replied. "I do. And I can tell you that he's a child prodigy. Believe it. And he's no child. He's nineteen. He's the coolest, most diabolical nineteen-year-old delinquent you've ever seen. Which is precisely the reason the captain ruled that you're to stay away from him. And he's right, too. Like always, almost, the captain is right."

"But if Sonny Blake identifies Biggs, we've got it made." I insisted. "I don't know why you can't *see* it. My God, you told me just a couple of hours ago that Blake is a known criminal. And last night, whatever else he did, he resisted an officer's lawful order to halt. All we have to do is make a deal with him. If he doesn't want to get locked up, he can identify Biggs. Otherwise, he's screwed."

Again Friedman heaved his deep, doleful sigh. "Look. For all we know, James Biggs could have this line tapped. And I'm only half kidding. This kid is a genius. So be nice. Come in by four-thirty. Come in before if you want to. Meanwhile, to keep yourself occupied, find the Esterbrook-Gaines murderer." He paused, then asked, "Is it *really* the butler?"

"No."

"All right. I'll see you at four-thirty. And stay loose, for God's sake. Smile."

I got back in the car, slammed the door again, and brusquely motioned for Canelli to get under way. We drove several blocks in silence before Canelli tentatively asked, "Is everything all right, Lieutenant?"

Briefly, I told him what Friedman had said.

"Well," Canelli said heavily, "I got to admit, Lieutenant, that I can see Lieutenant Friedman's point. I mean, I guess it's true that the farther you stay away from this James Biggs, the better it'll look for you. At the trial, I mean."

I sighed. "I suppose you're right, Canelli. But, dammit, if we ran our business the way the lawyers wanted, we'd never get the job done."

"Well, yeah," Canelli said dubiously. "I suppose so." He

turned into Grant Avenue. Jonathan Esterbrook's address was just a few blocks away. "Those lawyers sure don't like to get their hands dirty, like you said."

"They learn it in law school. You'd better get over to the right. It's in the next block."

"Oh. Right." He hastily glanced back, then turned. "What'd you take in college, Lieutenant?"

I snorted. "I majored in business administration. But I went to school to play football. There—" I pointed. "Park there. It's that big apartment building across the street."

"Jeeze, that's some place. Jonathan Esterbrook must be loaded. I wonder what old man Esterbrook did, that he made so much money?"

"I think he was in real estate." I got out of the car, locked the door and joined Canelli, walking across the street toward Jonathan Esterbrook's building. It was a spectacular glass-and-concrete high rise, newly built.

"That Peter Fry is a strange one," Canelli offered as we waited for the elevator. "The more you talk to him, the more you get the feeling that he might really have been someone once. You know what I mean? When I was talking to him, I kept remembering those old South Seas movies, where there's this drunken beachcomber who's really the son of a fancy English nobleman, or something." As we stepped into the elevator, Canelli was frowning. "What'd they call those guys, that their families get out of the way like that? There's a name for them."

"Remittance men."

Canelli brightened. "Yeah, that's it." Then, speaking seriously, he said, "You know, Lieutenant, you really do know a lot. I mean it. I guess that's what comes from going to college. Maybe I should've gone."

"You're doing all right, Canelli." We stepped out into a richly carpeted hallway. "With your luck, you'll make sergeant in a couple of years. Provided you study for the exam, instead of going to the movies with your girlfriend." I gestered to Esterbrook's door and rang the bell. "Here we are."

"I hear he's a fag," Canelli whispered.

I shrugged. "Everyone has his hang-ups."

Aftershock

The door opened on the second ring. I was facing a man in his late forties, medium build, medium height. He was dressed in a maroon velour turtleneck shirt and tight-fitting double-knit slacks, sharply flared. His graying hair was mod-cut, coyly combed forward over his forehead, Napoleon style. His face was an antic demon's, with bushy, upswept satanic eyebrows and an upcurved mouth to match. Beneath the black, bushy brows, his eyes were alive with a kind of outlandish, roguish vitality. But the flesh of his face was pale and flaccid, deeply lined with a plain pattern of depravity and self-indulgence.

"Ah—" Jonathan Esterbrook stood with one hand on his hip, looking me up and down. "The inspector calls. Right?"

I nodded. "That's right, Mr. Esterbrook. I'm Lieutenant Hastings, this is Inspector Canelli." Simultaneously, we showed him our identification folders. "Can we come in?"

"*Please.*" He stepped back, elaborately gesturing us inside with a long, low, dancing-master's sweep of his arm. Canelli and I found seats side by side on a luxuriously tufted sofa. Jonathan Esterbrook sat opposite, in a small velvet armchair. Plainly excited, he sat forward, perched on the edge of the chair. His knees were pressed together almost primly. His hands were tightly clasped, tremulous with anticipation.

"This is really very thrilling," he said. "If that shocks you, I'm sorry. But my sister just called to say that you might come by. Charles, of course, was livid at the idea. Charles is her husband. But I have to confess that I *couldn't* wait. Do you really think there's a possibility of foul play, Lieutenant?"

"It's not a possibility, Mr. Esterbrook. Your mother was murdered."

"I'm *aware* of that. But Grace said you suspect that someone in the family did it."

"That's not exactly true, Mr. Esterbrook. Our job is to look into every possibility. And, until we find the actual murderer, we have to look at everything." I paused, then added, "I'm glad the idea doesn't make you mad."

"Far from it. I'm intrigued. I'm sorry, of course, that Mother went the way she did. I hope she didn't suffer. But she lived a full life, as they say. She did what she wanted, and she wasn't afraid to raise a few eyebrows. In a way, I think I understood her. And I liked her, too. What little I saw of her, I liked her." He suddenly broke off, swallowing hard. His bright, puckish eyes momentarily lost their focus. But, almost immediately, he recovered himself, saying, "I wasn't scandalized, for instance, when she married Rupert. Everyone else was. Grace, all Mother's friends—they all squirmed. But not me. Of course—" He simpered briefly. "Of course, I can't exactly throw rocks."

"Do you think your mother and Rupert Gaines were happily married?"

He raised his shoulders in a slow, expressive shrug. "If you can define a happy marriage for me, Lieutenant, I'll answer the question. The point is, Rupert was getting what he wanted, and Mother was getting what *she* wanted. So the arrangement was a success."

"What did Rupert want?"

Again he languidly shrugged. "Money, of course. And Mother wanted the illusion that a younger man loved her. As nearly as I can see, both of them lived up to the bargain. So—ipso—the marriage was a success." He cocked his Satan-slanted eyebrows higher, smiling at me with a sudden, leering intimacy. "There are all kinds of arrangements between two people, Lieutenant. Believe me."

I eyed him thoughtfully for a moment, then decided to say, "You brought up the possibility that a member of the family could have been involved in the murder of your mother, Mr. Esterbrook. Do you think Rupert Gaines is the one?"

"I have no idea," he answered readily. "No suspicions. I'm merely titillated, waiting to see what's going to happen. Offhand, though, I'd say that Rupert doesn't have the guts to murder anyone. He's simply a gigolo. An amiable, reasonably pretty gigolo."

"I'm not so sure," I answered slowly. "He and Charles Carstairs were arguing about the will just a short while ago. Rupert has a considerable temper, it seems to me."

"Temper is one thing," he said, "guts is something else."

"What about your sister and her husband?"

"Hmm—" He pretended to consider the point, then slowly nodded. "That might be more of a possibility. My sister, of course, couldn't have actually done it—or planned it. Such a thing simply isn't done in polite society. And my sister's entire concern, you see, is the appearance of things. Literally, she lives for the moment she reads her name in the society columns. And Charles, of course, married her for her family's money—which he promptly proceeded to blow once Grace came into her inheritance. So, between the two of them—considering that, actually, Charles is essentially a mean, vicious type—I can see that, yes, they could be responsible for Mother's death. I don't *believe* it, necessarily. But I can see the *possibility* of it."

"What do you mean, exactly, when you say that Charles Carstairs blew your sister's inheritance?"

He shrugged, spreading his arms in a wide, theatrical gesture. "My father died ten years ago, as I'm sure you know. He left Grace and me a hundred thousand dollars apiece. That's a lot of money if you don't waste it—and if you water it and make it grow. But if you're supporting a fancy apartment in Pacific Heights and a summer place at Tahoe, and if you can't hold up your head unless you have a maid, then it doesn't last very long—especially if your husband doesn't seem to have the knack of making money grow."

I glanced around the apartment. It was small, but beautifully furnished—a luxury one-bedroom unit with a tiny kitchen and spectacular view of the bay and the Golden Gate Bridge. Monthly rental, probably five hundred dollars.

"You seem to have the knack of making money grow," I observed.

"I took my hundred thousand dollars and invested it in blue-chip stocks," he answered. "I kept my job. In fact, I kept it until last year."

"What kind of work does Charles Carstairs do?"

He grimaced. "He's an investment counselor, whatever that means. But, actually, he fancies himself a financier. He backs one scheme after another, mostly real estate. Usually he comes a cropper. A few years ago he made a little money in the market, but he soon lost it. Charles, you see, can't resist a tip. And if you play enough tips in the stock market, you're bound to lose money. In a way—" Esterbrook paused, frowning as he posed with his chin resting pensively on a forefinger. "In a way, you see, Grace and Charles are perfectly suited to each other. They're both concerned with the appearance of things, not the substance. Grace dreams of total social acceptance. Charles dreams of becoming rich and powerful—magically, without sweating. Both of them, of course, are fantasizing."

"It might happen now," I said quietly. "Your sister is about to become an heiress. You, too."

His smile was impish. "Don't forget Rupert, Lieutenant. And, for that matter, don't forget Peter Fry."

"I understand that Rupert made *his* money grow, too."

The impish smile twisted derisively. "Not Rupert. Susan Platt. In that partnership, if you'll pardon the expression, Susan has the balls. Actually, I have to admire Rupert. Whatever his faults, he had sense enough to set himself up beautifully. He's got an older woman to provide for him, and a young woman to take care of him."

"Does Susan Platt take care of Rupert?"

"I'd say so. Yes."

"Financially? Or sexually?"

He shrugged. "Both, I'd say. But that's just a guess. Actually, I suppose Rupert has a weak sex drive. Otherwise, he couldn't abide his relationship with my mother. Or, for that matter, with Susan Platt. A real stud wouldn't go for either woman— for different reasons, of course."

"You're a very good observer, Mr. Esterbrook."

"I know," he answered complacently. "Most homosexuals are very sensitive. It goes with the territory."

Momentarily taken aback, I couldn't think of a reply. Finally I asked, "Do you mind my asking what you did last night, Mr. Esterbrook?"

The too-bright sparkle came back into his eyes. "This is the part I've been waiting for," he breathed. "The grilling."

Wondering whether his strange sense of perverted titillation also went with the territory, I waited for him to continue.

"The answer, actually, is disgustingly simple. I was home all night. I didn't even go out to dinner, and I didn't see anyone, I'm afraid. I fixed myself an omelette and watched TV solidly from seven o'clock to ten. Then I went to bed—with a book," he added coyly. "I turned off the light about eleven-thirty. At quarter to two, Grace called. Period."

"When was the last time you were in your mother's house, Mr. Esterbrook?"

He grimaced. "I hate to tell you. I was trying to think this morning. It's been a year, anyhow."

"How about the garage?"

"The garage?"

"Yes. Have you, by any chance, been in her garage during the past few days?"

"My God," he breathed, sitting up straighter. "You're not kidding, are you?"

I didn't answer. I saw him swallow, then say, "N—no. I haven't been in her garage, either. Not for a year, anyhow."

"You're sure?" Asking the question, I eyed his wall-to-wall carpeting, wondering whether the lab could find traces of Kleen-Eeze. I was also wondering whether to ask him for permission to test his clothing and shoes. I decided against it. If he'd murdered her, he would have thrown everything away.

"You live alone, then," I said.

"I'm afraid so," he sighed. "For the moment, anyhow. I don't always. It's a fluid situation, you understand."

No one, then, could tell me whether any of his clothing was missing. I sat for a moment silently, wondering whether I'd forgotten anything. Finally I rose to my feet. Beside me, Canelli did the same. Rising with us, Jonathan Esterbrook said, "You haven't asked me about the chauffeur, Lieutenant. Peter Fry. He's an heir, too, you know."

"Are you suggesting him as a suspect?" I asked, looking at him closely.

"Not really. I—" He hesitated, momentarily flustered. "I was just wondering. Call it morbid curiosity."

I continued to stare at him, watching his confusion mount. On impulse, I decided to slip a wild card into the deck.

"At the moment," I answered slowly, "we don't consider Peter Fry a suspect. As a matter of fact, he could turn out to be a very important witness for us."

"A—" He licked at his lips. "An important witness?"

I nodded. "I thought you knew. Fry saw the murderer leaving the premises last night."

"But—" His hand flipped up in a quick, uncontrolled gesture of protest. "But he—he's a suspect himself. I—I don't see how you could trust him."

I turned deliberately away, walking to the door. "In this business," I said, "an eyewitness means everything. And, until we know differently, that's what Peter Fry is—an eyewitness." I turned the knob, opened the door and stepped out into the hallway. As Canelli followed me out, I turned back. Jonathan Esterbrook seemed to have shrunken inside his velour shirt. His face was suddenly bleak, no longer mischievously Satanslanted. He looked like an overdressed, over-the-hill homosexual, aging the hard way.

"Whoever killed my mother," he said softly, "I hope you find him. Or her."

"We'll find him," I answered. "Or her."

Eight

As the waitress gestured inquiringly with her coffee pot, Canelli asked, "Mind if I have another cup, Lieutenant? We got time?"

"Go ahead. I'll have some, too."

Canelli sipped noisily at his coffee, then asked, "What now, Lieutenant?"

I glanced at my watch. The time was 2:15 P.M. "I think we're going to split up," I said thoughtfully. "It's time we got this investigation organized."

Canelli nodded. "Right." Then, plainly concerned that he'd given the impression he thought we were disorganized, he said, "I mean, that's a good idea."

"I've told Culligan that I want him to get whatever he can and come down to the Hall between five and five-thirty. I checked with him while you were ordering lunch, and he's got some background information on the victim. He sent Sigler down to her bank to take care of the safe-deposit box and get a copy of the will. Sigler's going to check with the lawyer, too. Culligan, meanwhile, is going to reinterrogate Gaines, Peter Fry and Charlotte Young. Plus, he's going to keep checking the neighbors for gossip."

"That's good," Canelli said. He frowned thoughtfully. "You know, Lieutenant, you got me thinking, what you said to Jonathan Esterbrook when we were leaving."

"What'd I say?"

"Well, he said it first. 'Or her,' he said. And that got me to thinking about Charlotte Young."

"And?"

"Well, she certainly had the opportunity."

"But she doesn't have a motive."

"You never know with some of those black militants, though. I mean, some of them will give you the business just because you're white. And besides, she sure doesn't have an alibi."

"Neither do Charles Carstairs or his wife," I answered. "And that's where you come in."

"Me?"

"Right. I want you to check them out. Get as much as you can on what they were doing last night and come down to the Hall between five and five-thirty. You can call in for a black-and-white car. Don't worry if you can't get a lot from the Carstairs. I don't expect them to be very cooperative. Mainly, I want them to know that they're on the hook—that we aren't backing off just because Carstairs is throwing his weight around. Meanwhile, I'm going to interrogate Susan Platt. If she's Rupert Gaines's mistress, that could be Gaines's motive. I'd like to see what she says. Then I'm going down to the Hall."

"Can you see Gaines swinging the pipe?" Canelli asked, plainly doubtful.

"I don't know," I answered slowly. "I don't think he's the wilting violet that he seems. Plus, it doesn't take a tiger to hit a seventy-year-old woman on the head, especially if you can get close to her. Which, certainly, he could have. Oh, incidentally, you can tell the Carstairs that we think Fry eyeballed the murderer. See how that hits them."

"It sure seemed to hit Esterbrook."

"Yes," I said thoughtfully. "Yes, it sure did."

"Did you have an appointment with Miss Platt?" the receptionist asked. She was a nervous, narrowly built girl with stringy blond hair and large, anxious brown eyes.

"No. But if you tell her that I'm making some inquiries concerning the death of Mrs. Rupert Gaines, I think she'll see me."

"Oh. Yes. I'm—I'm sure she will. Just a moment." The receptionist bounded up from her desk and bolted to a door marked "S. Platt." A moment later the receptionist reappeared, beckoning me inside with an agitated flutter of her hand. Entering the office, I could feel the receptionist's tragic gaze following me as she breathed something about "poor Mister Gaines."

I introduced myself, then looked "S. Platt" over as we made preliminary small talk. She was still in her twenties—a small, slim girl, wound up tight. She moved with a taut, purposeful assurance, and spoke with flat, authoritative precision. Her eyes were quick and shrewd. Her face was a mannequin's: coldly sculptured, completely unrevealing. Softened, her face would be beautiful, I decided. But she never smiled. Her dark, glossy hair was pulled back close to her head; her expensive sweater modeled small, provocative breasts. As I watched her, I had the strong feeling that if Susan Platt went to bed with Rupert, it was Susan's idea.

"What can I do for you, Lieutenant Hastings?" As she asked the question, she lit a cigarette. Her lighter, I saw, was a gold Dunhill. Waiting for me to reply, she deftly bounced the expensive lighter up and down in her palm. Sitting behind her rosewood-and-chrome desk, she was completely at ease.

I decided to come directly to the point. Hopeful of putting her off balance, I spoke in a flat, official voice, looking her directly in the eye as I said, "Whenever a wife is murdered, it's our policy to check on the movements of the husband. I understand Mr. Gaines spent the evening with you last night. Is that right?"

The question seemed to amuse her. Lifting one cool mannequin's eyebrow, she said, "You're hoping my story will contradict Rupert's. Is that it?"

"Not necessarily. We don't root for one suspect over another, Miss Platt. We just get the information. The rest takes care of itself."

Still she seemed sardonically amused. "All you want are the facts. Right?"

I nodded. "That's it exactly."

"Well, the facts are that we had dinner together. At Monroe's. I guess we left the restaurant about nine or nine-thirty. We came back here for a drink. Rupert left a little before eleven, I suppose. At least, he was gone by the time the eleven o'clock news came on."

"Do you usually spend Tuesday nights together?" I asked.

Her eyes momentarily narrowed. She took a moment to consider, still bouncing the gold cigarette lighter in her hand. She caught the lighter with a deft, decisive masculine gesture.

"Probably every other Tuesday," she answered.

"And, of course, you see each other during the day."

"Why do you say that?"

"You're partners, aren't you?"

She nodded. "We're partners, yes. But I have my office here, at the downtown branch. Rupert has his office in the Stonestown Shopping Center. Out on Nineteenth Avenue. Actually, that's the reason that we get together after hours. We seldom see each other during working hours."

"I didn't realize that," I said, holding her eye.

Again she raised an indifferent eyebrow. Now, leaning forward, she deposited the lighter on the desk top with a small, sharp click. "Do you really think," she asked contemptuously, "that Rupert could have murdered his wife?"

"Do you think so?" I countered quietly.

"Definitely not. No way."

"Why're you so sure, Miss Platt?"

"It's simply not in Rupert's nature."

"You may be right. However, I've investigated hundreds of homicides. And I can tell you that almost anyone, under the proper circumstances, is capable of murder."

"Not Rupert," she said flatly. "Not murder."

"Have you talked to him today?" I asked.

She hesitated momentarily. Then: "Yes. He called this morning to tell me what happened."

"For business reasons?"

"Naturally, for business reasons," she snapped. "What're you getting at, anyhow?" The carefully contrived sophistication of her diction had slipped, revealing a hard, street-corner edge.

"What I'm getting at, Miss Platt, are rumors that you and Rupert Gaines are romantically involved."

Except for a glint of contempt in her dark, watchful eyes, her expression didn't change. "That's your business, I suppose —to listen to rumors."

"Is it true? Are you involved with each other?"

"What difference would it make, Lieutenant? Officially, I mean."

"We're talking about murder, Miss Platt. Premeditated murder. For premeditated murder, you look for motives. And a young man married to an older woman, in love with a younger woman, would have a motive. Especially if, when his wife died, he'd inherit a lot of money."

"*Are* we talking about premeditated murder? I thought she was murdered by someone who wanted her purse."

"Maybe. But I doubt it. The more I know about the case, the more I think the murder was planned. It wasn't committed for petty cash."

"Well," she retorted, "it wasn't committed for love, either. Not by Rupert, anyhow."

"For gain, then?"

She shrugged, at the same time leaning forward to grind out her cigarette in an outsize crystal ashtray. Then, straightening, she studied me for a long, deliberate moment before asking, "Have you talked with Rupert about this—this rumor you've picked up, that we're lovers?"

To myself, I smiled. She was smart, and could think on her feet. She didn't want to get caught in a contradiction.

"In this business," I said softly, "we take things one at a time."

"So if I deny it and Rupert admits it, then I'm on the hook. Right?" The street-corner harshness in her speech was plainer now. As Jonathan Esterbrook had said, Susan had the balls.

I smiled at her. "Right."

"The tricks of the trade."

"Right again."

"Then I suppose I may as well admit it, since it's the truth. But Rupert didn't kill her. Not for money or for love. And especially not for love."

"According to what you say, Rupert doesn't sound like much of a lover."

Her lips stirred, upcurving into a frosty smile. She was recovering her cool. "I didn't say that, Lieutenant."

"Did you make love last night?"

"No."

"Why not?"

She shrugged. "I suppose we weren't in the mood. Rupert can pretty much take it or leave it."

"You decide whether you'll make love."

Again she shrugged, glancing pointedly at her watch.

"I gather," I said, "that you make the decisions in business, too. Is that right?"

"I suppose so. Yes."

"You've got a pretty good thing going here." As I said it, I pitched my voice to an ironic note, deliberately trying to antagonize her. I glanced around her expensively furnished office. "How'd it start with you and Rupert?" I asked dryly. "In the office, or in bed?"

"It all started in the office," she answered sharply. "And that's where it'll end—if it ends." As she spoke, her hand was slowly, involuntarily clenching into a small, cruel fist. She had a temper, then. Balls, and a temper.

"When you start mixing business with bed," I observed, "you usually can't draw a line."

"Usually. Not always. It depends on what you're after. And I'm after money, Lieutenant, pure and simple. I was born on the wrong side of the tracks, as the saying goes. My father took off when I was in kindergarten and never came back. Every kid on my block had more money than I did. And I never forgot it."

"I can see that. But I still say that you can't separate bed and business."

"Have you ever tried, Lieutenant?" The contemptuous challenge was back in her voice.

I blinked momentarily. A brief, wincing backflash put me in an office similar to the one in which I now sat. The time was twelve years ago. I'd been a so-called public relations man on my father-in-law's payroll. But, really, I'd been nothing more

62

than a tour guide for important visitors who wanted to see the sights and talk pro football, my only real specialty. Sometimes the visitors had wanted girls. It had been my job to oblige.

"We're talking about you," I said. "Not me."

"No," she corrected coldly, "we're talking about Rupert."

"And you don't think Rupert is my man." I got suddenly to my feet and picked up my hat from the corner of her desk. I was anxious to leave; I wanted to see Friedman before the city attorney arrived at the Hall. "In that case," I said, "I may as well be going. If you think of anything that might help me, Miss Platt, give me a call." I placed my card in the center of her uncluttered desk, nodded and turned toward the door.

Nine

The time was almost three-thirty when I started the engine and pulled away from the curb in front of the Gaines Travel Service. I'd driven less than a block when a static-blurred "Inspectors Eleven" call came over the radio.

I flipped the switch, acknowledging the call.

"You're to call 824-4076, Lieutenant," the dispatcher said laconically. "Repeat, 824-4076."

It was Ann's number. Apprehensively I asked, "Is there any message?"

"No sir. Lieutenant Friedman cleared this broadcast."

I pulled into the next service station and used a phone booth. Ann answered on the first ring.

"Frank?"

"Yes. What's wrong?"

"I—" Her voice caught. "I just got home. And—and someone's been here."

"What's happened, Ann?"

"Well, I—I just got home, about ten minutes ago. And at first, I—I didn't know anything was wrong. But then I went into the bedroom. And—" She broke off, fighting for control. I could hear her drawing a deep, tremulous breath. "And I—I saw that the whole room was torn up. And the first thing I saw was what he—he'd written on the mirror. He'd used one of my lipsticks. And he—he'd written 'Death.' It was—" This time, she couldn't continue.

"Now listen to me, Ann. Just listen and don't talk. After what happened last night, we detailed a cruiser—an unmarked car—to keep an eye on you. They're parked outside your flat, somewhere. Two men. If you can't spot them, just stand in front of your house. Wave your hand, or something. They'll come to you. Do you understand?"

"Y—yes."

"Are Dan and Billy home yet?"

"No."

"All right. Do as I tell you now. I'll be there in ten minutes. Meanwhile, when you talk to the two men outside, tell them to contact me on Tach two. Do you understand that? It's a radio channel. Tach two."

"Tach two. Yes."

"Right. Go outside now. I love you."

I heard her sob suddenly. "I—I'm sorry to bother you, darling. But hurry."

"I will. Hang up now." I waited for the click, then strode to my car. I'd driven for five minutes before I heard a voice on Tach two saying, "Lieutenant Hastings? This is Inspector Galton. General Works."

"Is everything secure?" I asked.

"Yessir. My partner and I are inside the Haywood premises. Everything's secure."

"All right. I'll be there in less than five minutes. Meanwhile, I want you to get a fingerprint crew out there, my authority. Clear?"

"Yessir."

"All right. I'll see you in a few minutes."

I took the trouble to park legally in Ann's block, unwilling to attract attention. As I was walking to her flat, I saw her younger son, Billy, approaching from the opposite direction. He was carrying school books and seemed to be kicking an imaginary soccer ball as he walked. He was eleven years old—

a good-looking, bright-eyed boy with strong opinions, sudden enthusiasms and a good pair of football shoulders.

"Hey, Frank. Hi."

"Hi, Billy. How's it going?"

"Fine. Just fine."

We'd arrived at the Haywoods' sidewalk together. I reached into my pocket and took out my billfold, extracting two dollars. "Listen, Billy, I promised your mother I'd pick up a quart of chocolate-chip ice cream at O'Connors, but I forgot. Would you mind doing it for me? And get a cone for yourself." I handed him the two dollars, at the same time reaching for his books. "I'll take these in for you."

His glance was speculative, but he nodded agreement. He handed over the books and walked away briskly. I'd bought fifteen minutes, maybe twenty. I knocked on the Haywoods' front door, then turned the knob and went inside. The family lived in a five-room flat, on the ground floor. I'd often thought about the crime statistics relating to ground-floor flats. But because the place was home for Ann, I'd never mentioned my misgivings.

She came into the hallway to meet me. Without speaking, I took her into my arms and pulled her close. I could feel her shudder as she buried her face deep in the hollow of my shoulder.

"I met Billy outside," I whispered. "I sent him for ice cream."

She sniffled, nodded and drew resolutely away. Blinking, she managed to smile. Glancing over her shoulder, I saw Inspector Galton standing in the hallway outside her bedroom, conspicuously looking the other way. I drew Ann into the living room.

"What happened?" I spoke in a low, quiet voice. I wanted an answer—fast. The time was five minutes to four. In thirty-five minutes I was due downtown, to meet with Rankin. Even using my flashing red light, it was a fifteen-minute drive.

"I—" She shook her head sharply, at the same time lifting her chin. Her small, determined mouth was firmly set. It was a willful, stubborn expression—one I seldom saw, but always respected. She was angry—at herself. Her gray eyes steadied as she began to speak. "I got home about quarter after three, I guess. Maybe a little earlier. When I—I went into the bedroom, I saw that it was completely torn up. I told you that on the phone. The—" She faltered. But, immediately, her chin came up again. "The first thing I saw was the—the mirror. He'd written 'Death.' I told you that, too. But, really, that wasn't the worst part. It was the—the knife."

"The knife?"

She swallowed hard, then nodded. "It was from the kitchen —that big butcher knife with the bone handle. It was stuck into the pillow." She paused, then added, "Into *my* pillow."

She had a double bed, with two pillows. She always slept on the left side—the opposite side, she'd once told me, from the side she'd slept on when she was married.

"Did you touch the knife?" I asked.

"No." At the thought, she momentarily closed her eyes. Then, speaking steadily: "I knew enough not to touch it. But then I—I started to look around the room. I was stunned, I guess. In shock, actually. But I remember that I wanted to see what else he'd done. And then I—I saw my underclothes."

Involuntarily, I was swearing to myself.

"He'd apparently taken the knife," she said, speaking very slowly, "and he'd slashed all my underthings. He'd done it very—very precisely. He—" She glanced over her shoulder toward the hallway door, then lowered her voice. "He'd slashed them all in the same way. The—the panties, he'd slashed right at the—the crotch. And he'd slashed the—the bras in the middle of each cup." She drew a deep, unsteady breath, still fighting for control. She blinked, biting her lip. "Right in the middle," she finished.

I waited a moment, then asked quietly, "Is that all?"

She slowly, silently nodded.

"Then you called me."

"Yes."

I glanced at my watch. The time was ten minutes after four; my time was running out. I reached forward, dropping my hands on her shoulders. It was a purposefully bluff gesture, at arm's length.

"I've got to go in just a few minutes. I'll be back later—this evening. But now I've got to go. Those two inspectors—Galton and his partner—will stay right with you. So there's nothing to worry about. A fingerprint crew will be coming in a half-hour or so. Galton will tell them what to do. When's Dan due home?"

"I—I'm not sure. Not until dinner time, probably. He's going out for the swimming team, at high school."

"Then you'd better figure what you're going to tell Billy. If I were you, I'd handle the whole thing casually. Just tell him it's a nut. Tell him there's no real danger. Which there isn't."

She nodded obediently.

"I'm sorry," I said. "But I've got to go. I'm going to talk to Galton, then go out the back way. As soon as I can, I'll either phone you or come back. But it probably won't be until seven o'clock, at least. Do you understand?"

Again she nodded meekly. Tentatively, like a child, she took a step toward me. I took her quickly in my arms, whispering into the hollow of the shoulder that she mustn't worry. I kissed her once, hard, then turned abruptly away. Galton was waiting for me in the hallway.

"Where's your partner?" I asked.

"He's in the car outside."

"Do you know how entrance was effected?"

He pointed down the hallway toward the flat's back door. "There's jimmy marks. To me, it looks like he jimmied the outside service entrance, in front, then came along the passageway to the back of the house. Both doors are easy, and the back door wasn't bolted."

Stifling an impatient exclamation at someone's carelessness, I said, "I've got to go down to the Hall. I want you to get everything you can here, then call me at the Hall between five-thirty and six. Are you detailed to stay here until you're relieved?"

"Yessir."

"When's your shift over?"

"Ten-thirty."

"All right. I'll fix it with your duty officer. Do the best you can, Galton. These people are friends of mine. *Good* friends."

"I—" He hesitated. "I know."

I nodded. "Good. I'll be talking with you between five-thirty and six. Don't call from here. Right?"

"Yessir."

I clapped him lightly on the shoulder. "Thanks a lot, Galton. I appreciate it." I turned, took a moment to survey the wrecked bedroom, then drew my handkerchief from my pocket as I carefully opened the back door. Two minutes later, I was in the car. As I pulled away from the curb, I saw Billy in the rear mirror. To myself, I smiled. For once, I'd out-maneuvered Ann's younger son. It didn't happen often.

Ten

"You're cutting it pretty thin," Friedman commented, staring at his watch.

"Is Rankin here yet?"

"He sure is. I've got him stashed in Conference Room A. He's fidgeting." Friedman hurried me toward the elevator. "What's with Ann?"

"I'll tell you later." I punched the elevator button.

"Do you think her problem is connected with James Biggs?"

"What'd *you* think?" I asked angrily.

"Now, listen—" Friedman laid a hand on my arm as we stepped into the empty elevator. "Don't go off half-cocked."

"Meaning what?"

"Meaning that, number one, I want you to keep your temper while you're talking with Rankin. And, number two, I don't think you should tell him about this business today at Ann's. It could've been anyone—a coincidence."

"Is he going to let us have Sonny Blake identify Biggs?"

Friedman sighed. "I don't know, Frank. I doubt it. But I'm telling you that, if you're cool, we can get to Biggs through the back door. The captain and I have already talked about it. If you get Rankin breathing on us, though, it'll all hit the fan. So, take a long, deep breath. Get that determined, square-jawed look off your face. It always means trouble—usually for you."

"It could mean trouble for Biggs, too. That's what he needs—a little trouble."

"Listen, Frank—" His voice dropped to a lower, more purposeful note. "Cool it. Give your friends a chance to help you."

We were leaving the elevator. Ahead, two doors down on our left, was Conference Room A.

"It's not going to help," Friedman said, "being late. A lawyer's time, you realize, is more valuable than ours. Did you know that?" He was bantering, trying to lighten the mood between us.

Grunting in reply, I pushed open the conference room's deeply paneled oak door. George Rankin sat hunched thick-shouldered over his attaché case. He was a somberly dressed man whose black-framed glasses and dark, glossy hair accentuated the unhealthy pallor of his face. He looked like a con, just out of prison. His hands, too, were very pale—also matted with black hair. I'd once tried to imagine Rankin naked, visualizing his paunchy, flaccid body mottled with pelts of black fur.

"Well," he said heavily, gesturing us to chairs. "You're a little late."

"A traffic jam," I said. "Sorry."

"I thought that's why you fellows had sirens."

Neither Friedman nor I commented.

"What I wanted to talk about," Rankin said ponderously, "is the matter of the Nancy Frazer–James Biggs case. I understand you have some suspicion that James Biggs may have hired someone—a petty hoodlum, as I understand it—to keep track of you. Is that right?"

As I was about to reply, Friedman spoke. "I don't know whether 'keep track of' is exactly accurate," he said mildly. "If our suspicions are correct, Biggs supplied Blake with a so-called shotgun mike—a very sophisticated piece of electronic surveillance equipment. The going price for shotgun mikes is about five hundred dollars. Sonny Blake was using the mike to keep Lieutenant Hastings and Ann Haywood, his friend, under surveillance for a period of two months, off and on."

"Can you prove that?"

"We have Blake's word for it. What happened, apparently, was that the two of them met in a bar—a gay bar—about two months ago. Biggs asked Blake if he'd like to make an easy fifty dollars. No risk. He—"

"Excuse me," Rankin interrupted. "But did Sonny Blake identify James Biggs by name?"

"No. They didn't use names. But the man he describes fits Biggs."

"Um. Go ahead, please."

"Thanks," Friedman said dryly. "The proposition was simple. Blake was to stake out Lieutenant Hastings' house—very much as we'd stake out someone, I gather. He'd wait for Lieutenant Hastings to come home from work. He'd keep an eye on him until he went to bed. Then, next day, he'd report to Biggs. All for fifty bucks, twenty-five going in, twenty-five when the report was made. It was all very businesslike. This happened maybe once a week, for about a month. Then, about a—"

"Excuse me again." Rankin turned to me. "During that time, were you aware that anyone was following you, Lieutenant?"

"No, I wasn't."

"No suspicions?"

"None."

"So it wasn't until last night—approximately two months after the surveillance began—that you realized anything was wrong. Is that correct?"

"That's correct."

"Hmm—" Rankin's thick black brows came together in a judicious frown. He waved for Friedman to continue.

"About a month ago, as I understand it," Friedman said, "the surveillance switched from Lieutenant Hastings to Ann Haywood. Ann is, ah, Frank's friend. And, about that time, Biggs came up with this shotgun-mike wrinkle. Also, maybe for the first time, Biggs probably took an active part in this game he was playing."

"How do you know?" Rankin asked.

"A shotgun mike is normally used in connection with a tape recorder. It transmits whatever it picks up to a radio receiver, which is connected to a tape recorder. And the receiver's got to be close by. Not more than a half-block away, usually."

"So James Biggs was actually nearby, last night?"

"Probably. Of course, we aren't absolutely sure. Blake didn't see him. However, it would've been fifty bucks wasted if he wasn't somewhere in the neighborhood with his tape recorder. Not to mention five hundred dollars wasted, for the shotgun mike."

"Um—" Rankin was chewing on his lower lip.

"We've already got Sonny Blake for illegal surveillance and resisting arrest," I said. "If he identifies Biggs, we've got them both."

"What if he fails to identify Biggs?" Rankin asked.

"All we've got to do is offer him a lesser charge, provided he makes the identification. You could work it out with the D.A."

"That's all very well," Rankin said. "But the question still stands. Suppose, just for the sake of argument, that we offer Blake a deal. Suppose he accepts. Then suppose he doesn't make the identification. What then?"

I spread my hands. "Then he doesn't get the deal. He's back inside. And Biggs is in the clear. Where's the percentage for Blake?"

"Let me pose you a problem, Lieutenant." Rankin leaned back in his chair, plainly about to play intellectual games with me. "Let's assume that James Biggs is worried about whether he's going to win his suit against you—and us. Let's suppose that his lawyer has advised him that his chances are pretty slim. So now let's suppose that he figures out a way to maneuver us into harassing him. He tells Blake to get himself caught and to describe him, Biggs, to us. Biggs knows we'll put him in a line-up. Then, for maybe a thousand dollars, Blake doesn't make the identification. So we look like we're harassing Biggs, just before his case comes to trial. His claim for damages, if you remember, is a million and a half dollars. A thousand dollars would be pretty cheap insurance if it got Biggs closer to a million and a half."

"That's ridiculous," I said. "Things just don't happen like that. You're building Biggs up to be some kind of a—an evil genius. *Both* of you." I aimed the last thrust at Friedman, whose eyes rolled forlornly up toward the ceiling as he slowly shook his head.

"In connection with this case," Rankin said stolidly, "I've taken two depositions from Biggs. I've also been in consultation with Lieutenant Friedman concerning Biggs. And we both agree that he's certainly evil—and very probably a genius." He shot me a patronizing look. "You've never met Biggs, have you?"

"Not yet," I answered shortly, glancing pointedly at Friedman. "I've been told to stay away from him."

"Well, naturally," Rankin answered. "That's quite right. You're the last person in the world who should have anything to do with Biggs."

"Listen, counselor—" I leaned toward him intently. "I have a confession to make. I wasn't delayed by a traffic jam. I was delayed because I had to go by Ann Haywood's place. Someone broke into her flat and wrote 'Death' on her mirror, and tore up her room and took a butcher knife to her underclothing. Then he left the knife stuck in her pillow. Now—" I paused, to compel his close attention. "Now, I care what happens to Ann. I care a lot. I wouldn't want her harmed. And I can tell you that sticking a knife in someone's pillow isn't very far from sticking it in the person. That's a professional opinion, Counselor. I deal with creeps like Biggs every day. And you can be damn sure that I'm not going to subject Ann to—"

"What you're doing, you see," Rankin interrupted, "is falling into exactly the kind of trap I've described. Chapter and verse."

"Maybe," I answered evenly, "maybe not. But I think we'd better start setting a trap for Biggs, instead of worrying that he's setting a trap for us. Biggs is just one man. He's not even a man. He's a nineteen-year-old kid who apparently used to pull wings off flies. Well, as I said, people like him are my business. And if he can—"

"Now, listen, Hastings—" Behind the heavy black-framed glasses, Rankin's eyes popped angrily. "There's no point in getting yourself all worked up. We've got to—"

"Well, I'm sorry, but I *am* worked up. It's about time we—"

"If you think, for one moment, that I'm going to let you—or anyone—jeopardize my defense against a suit for a million and a half dollars, Lieutenant, you're wrong. Completely wrong.

And that's not to mention your defense, which you should be thinking about, for God's sake."

For a moment we sat staring wrathfully at each other. I heard Friedman sigh deeply.

"He's right, Frank," Friedman said quietly. "You should listen to him. The first thing for you to worry about is defending yourself. That's the first thing for *all* of us to worry about. After you're off the hook, we can go after Biggs. We'll nail him, too—and nail him good. But now isn't the time. And you know it just as well as I do."

As I turned my baleful gaze on Friedman, Rankin asked me, "Do you have a lawyer yet?"

"No," I answered shortly.

"Well, you'd better get one. And you'd better have him contact me so that we can coordinate our defenses. The trial date is only two months away, you know."

"I know."

"Meanwhile, I'd like to review with you the Nancy Frazer–James Biggs case from a legal point of view, and outline our line of defense."

Sullenly, I said nothing. I watched him shuffle through a sheaf of papers, clear his throat and tilt his head up to the correct bifocal angle.

"Of course," he said, "you're aware of the, ah, initial situation. Two years ago a detail of three detectives under your command was engaged in a running gun battle with an escaping fugitive. A ricocheting bullet struck Mrs. Frazer in the spine, paralyzing her from the waist down. The police board of inquiry established that the, ah, offending bullet came from a police weapon because of the angle of fire. However, it was impossible to determine which weapon fired the shot because the bullet was mangled when it ricocheted. Everyone agrees, though, that the three men under your command fired a total of five shots. You, yourself, fired none. However, since you were in command, the civil suit brought on behalf of Nancy Frazer named you, charging negligence." Rankin glanced up at me. "So far, we're in agreement on the facts, are we not?"

I silently nodded.

"All right. Good." Rankin nodded in return. We were friends again—friendly enemies. "Now, of course, it gets tricky. Six months ago, as we all know, Mrs. Frazer died. The cause of death was plain—a reaction between alcohol and barbiturates, a common enough occurrence. The subsequent investigation—" Rankin frowned, pawing at his papers until he found the right one. "The subsequent investigation revealed the following facts. First, Mrs. Frazer had a pattern of excessive drinking that antedated her paralysis. That point, of course, is vital. Second, death was caused by a barbiturate dosage roughly three times that prescribed by Mrs. Frazer's doctor. *That* point, too, is vital. When you put the two points together, the conclusion is inescapable. If Mrs. Frazer hadn't been a heavy drinker, and if she hadn't taken a barbiturate overdose, whether accidentally or willfully, she'd be alive today. The prosecution, of course, will contend that, first, she wouldn't have been taking the barbiturates if she hadn't been injured by a police bullet. They'll also claim that death was accidental, not willful. That latter point, as I'm sure you realize, Lieutenant, is absolutely essential to the prosecution's case. If Mrs. Frazer's death was willful—suicide—then Biggs can hardly have a claim on us for damages resulting from her death. However, if she died accidentally, their case is stronger —*much* stronger. So our defense is helped immeasurably by the finding of the coroner's jury, ruling that she died by her own hand. They didn't quite say suicide. They seemed to feel, as I understand it, that she became befuddled by drink and took an overdose of the barbiturate. That happens with great frequency. Of course, for our purposes, an out-and-out ruling of suicide would have been preferable. Still, we can—"

"There's another possibility," Friedman interrupted quietly. "There's the possibility that James Biggs did her in. He could've waited for her to get drunk, then slipped her a triple barbiturate. What about that?"

Rankin's broad, shapeless nose wrinkled distastefully. "That, of course, was never proven. So I—"

"Either her husband or her son had to've given her the stuff," Friedman said. "The husband says he didn't do it, and I be-

lieve him. He's not exactly the homicidal type. That leaves
James Biggs."

Rankin frowned. "The point is, Lieutenant, that Biggs
denies it. He claims that he provided his mother with her
regular dosage. However, for the three days preceding her
death, he didn't actually see her take the barbiturates. So the
supposition is that she saved up her dosages. That's where the
possibility of suicide comes in, you see. It's—"

"For God's sake," I interrupted, "all we've got to do is make
the kid admit he gave her a triple dose. It should be easy
enough. All we've got to do is count the goddamn pills. All it
takes is a little arithmetic. We can prove that—"

Rankin shook his head. "The time to have done that,
Lieutenant, was six months ago. Not now." He looked inquiringly at Friedman.

"Unhappily," Friedman sighed, "assuming the kid killed her,
he was too smart for us. He flushed the remaining pills down
the toilet before the police arrived—responding to his call,
incidentally. He says he did it in a fit of boyish grief. And as
long as he sticks to his story, there's nothing we can do. There's
absolutely no proof. And no way of getting proof, either. For
one thing, there's the question of motive. We can't—"

"What'd you mean, a question of motive?" I interrupted
hotly. "Christ, he had all the motive in the world. If she's alive,
and she wins the suit, *she* gets the money. If she's dead, *he*
sues. *He* gets the money. What's so complicated about that?"

"Simply that the death of Nancy Frazer appeared—or was
made to appear—like either suicide or, conceivably, murder,"
Rankin answered. "Either way, Biggs loses. So where's the
motive? He damaged his chances, in the long run."

"Sure he damaged his chances—in hindsight. But that just
means that Biggs isn't a lawyer. Going in, he didn't know he
was hurting himself. He thought he'd be better off with her
dead. To me, that's obvious. He—"

"What he's trying to tell you, Frank," Friedman said quietly,
"is that now it's too late to try and nail Biggs for anything.
God knows, at the time, I tried. I leaned on that kid like I
never leaned on anyone. But he just leaned right back, hard.
In your words, he's an evil genius—and don't forget it. So now,

if we lean on him, it's going to look like police harassment—like we're trying to intimidate him into dropping the lawsuit." He turned to Rankin. "Isn't that right, Counselor?"

"Definitely. I'm certain that his lawyer is going to try to prove municipal collusion. Therefore, any harassment—any contact with Biggs—would play right into their hands. It would—"

"Not if we can prove that Biggs is harassing Ann and me," I retorted. "And, especially, not if we can prove that he murdered his mother."

Rankin looked appealingly at Friedman, then consulted his watch. "I'm sorry," he said, fussily arranging his papers and dropping them into his attaché case. "It's after five. I've got to be going." Plainly irritated, he snapped the case shut and rose to his feet. He stood looking down at me, frowning darkly. "A million and a half dollars is a lot of money, Lieutenant Hastings," he said solemnly. "It might not be a problem to you, because you probably don't have it. But it'd be one hell of a problem to the city and county of San Francisco." He lifted his attaché case from the table and strode to the door.

Eleven

"Well," Friedman said, slumping into my visitor's chair. "You really screwed up."

"I never liked that pompous bastard."

"Nevertheless, he's got a good point. Several good points, in fact. And, if I were you, I'd—"

My phone rang. It was Galton, reporting from a phone booth in Ann's neighborhood.

"I think I might have a description of the one who did it, Lieutenant. It turns out that Mrs. Haywood's oldest son didn't leave the house until about noon because on Wednesdays he doesn't have to be at high school until one o'clock. And, at about two P.M., a boy who lives next door and was home sick observed a man dressed like a repairman working at the back door of the Haywood flat, like he was jimmying it. This boy is only nine years old, but he seems like a pretty good observer. And, besides, it all fits. The time and everything, I mean. When the Haywood boy left for school, nothing in the flat was disturbed."

"What's the description of the suspect?"

"Slim. Maybe a hundred thirty pounds. Dark-blond hair, fairly long, but not real long. A pale complexion. The kid mentioned it twice, how pale the suspect appeared. Young, I'd say. Maybe twenty. It's hard, you know, to get children to be accurate about ages. But I took quite a bit of time with this kid next door, pointing out people going by on the street and ask-ing him to rate the suspect's age according to the age of passers-by. And I think twenty is a good guess. The suspect was dressed in one of those dark-green twill jacket-and-trouser combinations, like a TV repairman, for instance, would wear. He was even carrying a little metal toolbox."

"Anything else? Any fingerprints on the knife?"

"Not that I could see. It looked like it'd been wiped. The fingerprint crew found lots of other prints around the room, of course. I guess you'll be hearing from the lab crew direct, though."

"You're going to stake the place out until ten o'clock, is that right?"

"Yessir."

"Good. I'll arrange for relief. And I'll be around myself, later on. Thanks." I hung up the phone and turned to face Friedman. He was staring at me with a wary, go-slow expression.

"Is James Biggs slim?" I asked. "About a hundred thirty pounds, very pale complexion, medium-long dark-blond hair?"

Reluctantly, Friedman nodded. "So it *was* him," he said thoughtfully. "Son of a bitch."

"Did you ever doubt it?"

"I guess I didn't," he answered slowly. "Not really. The older I get, though, the more I'm amazed at the power of wishful thinking."

For a moment we stared at each other silently, each of us trying to calculate the extent of the other's determination. Finally, speaking very quietly, I said, "What I'd like from you, Pete, is a complete rundown on James Biggs—his background, his record, everything. I'd like to know whether, in your opin-ion, he's capable of violence. I'd also like . . ."

Canelli materialized in the glass door of my office. I'd for-gotten that I'd ordered him to report at about five-thirty. Im-patiently, I beckoned him inside.

"What've you got, Canelli?" I asked. "Make it quick, will you?"

"Oh, sure, Lieutenant." Standing just inside the door, shift-ing his weight from one foot to the other, he recited, "I didn't get much from the neighbors, but I did get a chance to talk with Mr. Carstairs. He seemed to have calmed down from what he was out at the Gaines place. He'd just come from the coroner's, and maybe that cooled him off a little. Anyhow, I got a chance to ask him about where he was last night, and everything, without getting him too hot."

"And?"

"Well, it seems like he and Mrs. Carstairs went to a party last night. It was a dinner party, he said. Really a buffet, it turns out. They left for the party about seven-thirty. Then, about ten-thirty, Carstairs left the party—alone."

"Alone?"

"Right. Alone. I had the very strong feeling that they had some kind of an argument at the party. I couldn't quite get it straight. All Carstairs would say was that he wanted to leave early because he was tired, and his wife didn't. So he took the car and left. He got home about eleven, he says, and went right to sleep—in the spare room. He doesn't know when his wife got home. Or so he says."

"Who else was in the house except Carstairs and his wife?"

"Just the two kids. Two girls, age fourteen and sixteen. I didn't get a chance to talk to them yet."

"What about Mrs. Carstairs? Did you talk to her?"

"No, she's been out all day, making the funeral arrangements. The way I get it, they've got it worked out that she and Carstairs are going to make the arrangements, after all. Gaines has bowed out, except for some reason he's determined to select the funeral dress. Jonathan isn't interested in doing anything but going to the funeral."

I considered a moment, then said slowly, "You did a good job, Canelli. Do you have any plans for this evening?"

"Not really, Lieutenant. I mean, Gracie and I were going to go to a movie, maybe. But the same show's on tomorrow."

"Well, then, I'd like to have you keep on the Carstairs. Especially, interview Mrs. Carstairs. Whatever you're doing, you seem to be doing it right. Find out what she did last night, and what their two girls heard. Teen-agers don't sleep all that soundly. They might've heard something."

Canelli nodded. "I was thinking the same thing, Lieutenant."

"Before you go back to their house, though, I want you to

check with the lab. I've been meaning to do it, but I haven't had the time. Find out what they've discovered at the scene of the crime. Particularly, find out whether they think that Kleen-Eeze, plus the spilled oil, would stick to the suspect's shoes in sufficient quantities to show up on his carpet at home, assuming he ran down the alleyway and got into his car and drove directly home. I think it would show up, and I think it's something we should be checking. The Kleen-Eeze thing isn't going to do us much good where members of the Gaines household are concerned, but if we found Kleen-Eeze on Jonathan's carpet, for instance, or the Carstairs' carpet, we'd really have something. By the way, did you ask Carstairs whether he'd been in the Gaines's garage during the past two days?"

Canelli sheepishly dropped his eyes. "Jeeze, I forgot, Lieutenant."

"That's all right, Canelli. So did I. Make sure you ask him, though. And ask Mrs. Carstairs, too." I gestured to the door, dismissing him. "You'd better get down to the lab before they all go home. I'll see you in the morning. Nine o'clock."

"Yessir. Right." He left the office quickly. Canelli was never at ease reporting in a superior's office.

"The plot thickens," Friedman observed. "It sounds like you're getting results."

Seeing Culligan making for my office door, I didn't reply, but instead beckoned Culligan inside.

Nodding to Culligan, Friedman said to me, "You run your investigations very smoothly, Lieutenant. Everyone is reporting like parts of a well-oiled machine." He said it amiably— trying, I thought, to ease the strain of our differences concerning James Biggs.

"What've you got, Culligan?" I asked. "Make it brief, will you? Something else's come up."

Culligan, the most laconic man on the homicide squad, didn't need to be urged. "I just heard from Sigler by phone. He's at the victim's lawyer's office. Sigler saw copies of both the old will and the new will. The new will was unsigned, just like Carstairs said. In fact, according to Sigler, Carstairs got the information on the new will from Rodgers, the lawyer. That's unethical. For the lawyer, I mean. Anyhow, according to the original will"—Culligan consulted his notebook—"Peter Fry got five thousand dollars. Rupert Gaines got ten thousand plus full equity in his business, which is probably worth a fair amount of money. The rest is to be divided between Jonathan Esterbrook and Grace Esterbrook Carstairs."

"What's the size of the estate? Any idea?"

"Over a million dollars. After Sigler leaned on the lawyer a little, for divulging the contents of the new will to Charles Carstairs, the lawyer suddenly became cooperative about estimating the size of Flora's estate. He says that the house, which is free and clear, is probably worth about a hundred fifty thousand. Her stocks and bonds are worth—" Culligan's prominent Adam's apple moved up and down in his scrawny throat, as if the mention of so much money had caused him to salivate. "They're worth a little more than a million dollars, according to Rodgers."

"What about the new will?" I asked. "Why wasn't it signed?"

"Well, again, it looks like Carstairs was right. Rodgers wouldn't give an opinion, but it sure looks to me like that new will could've been a blind, to keep Rupert happy. The victim and her husband went to Rodgers' office about three months ago, and the victim outlined how she wanted the will changed. Rodgers wrote it up about a week later and notified the victim that it was ready for her signature. But she never came in. And, what's more, she told him that he wasn't supposed to discuss the new will with Rupert."

"But he *did* discuss it with Carstairs," Friedman said thoughtfully.

"Right."

"So what we've got," Friedman said softly, frowning slightly as he stared off, "is Rupert thinking he was in for half a million dollars, more or less. And we've also got Carstairs, who knew Rupert *wasn't* in—at least not until the new will was signed."

"Right again."

"In fact," Friedman said, "Carstairs thought his wife was in—for something over half a million. He *knew* she was in—at least until the new will was signed."

Culligan nodded.

"Did Rodgers say why he gave Carstairs the information about the two wills?" I asked.

"Not in so many words, according to Sigler. I questioned him pretty carefully over the phone just now," Culligan answered. "And what happened, apparently, was that Rodgers was—is—Carstairs' lawyer, too. And the information just slipped out, according to Rodgers, in casual conversation."

"I'll bet," Friedman put in laconically.

A moment of thoughtful silence passed before Culligan asked me, "What'd you hear on the street, Lieutenant? Anything?"

I shrugged. "Nothing." I looked inquiringly to Friedman, who also shrugged.

"It always takes a while," Friedman said, "for General Works to get under way. First they have to find some hood who's spitting on the sidewalk so they can offer him immunity in exchange for fingering a murderer." He shook his head. "Those General Works guys practically sleep with their suspects. It's obscene."

"So what now?" I asked Culligan. "What'd you think?"

He spread his hands indifferently, at the same time glancing at the clock. Culligan's wife complained loudly whenever he wasn't home in time for dinner. "If I was you, Lieutenant," he said finally, "I'd let the suspects stew for a while. This chauffeur, for instance. Fry. He's got something on his mind, but I can't figure what. And the maid, Charlotte Young, is starting to act like some kind of a—a radical agitator, or something, coming on with all that Black Panther crap and saying that, sure as hell, there's a murderer loose."

"What about Rupert Gaines?"

Culligan frowned. "I can't figure him. He's trying to play the part of the bereaved husband, but he's not very good at it. I don't see him hitting her over the head, but I could be wrong. A half a million dollars is a lot of money. Even ten thousand is a lot, plus a business free and clear." He glanced again at the clock.

"It doesn't sound like we can do much tonight," I said, glad to end the conversation. "Let's let it stew until tomorrow. If enough of them get mad at each other and worry about what the other one's thinking and doing, maybe we'll turn up something." I gestured dismissal. "I'll see you at nine tomorrow, Culligan."

"Right." He nodded to Friedman, turned and left the office without a word.

"I'd sure like to see Culligan getting a few more laughs," Friedman observed.

I smiled perfunctorily, then said, "What about James Biggs, Pete? What's the rundown?"

He eyed me steadily for a long, silent moment before saying, "I've been thinking about it while you were talking with Canelli and Culligan. And I want to tell you again, Frank, to let your friends help you."

"How can my friends help me?" I retorted. "Rankin is going to talk to the city attorney, and the city attorney's going to talk to the D.A., and the D.A.'s going to talk to the chief, and the chief is going to talk with Captain Kreiger, who's going to talk to me. Anyone who approaches Biggs is going to be in trouble. So if anyone's going to get into trouble, it might as well be me."

"Your reasoning is great," Friedman said. "But your conclusion is crappy."

"What'm I supposed to do? Wait until Biggs gets a traffic ticket?"

"No," he answered. "Just wait. Period. I'll give you the rundown on Biggs. As a friend, I'll give it to you. But I want you to promise me that you won't make any move toward Biggs tonight. Promise me you'll wait until tomorrow and then talk to me before you decide anything."

We eyed each other through another long, stern moment of silence. Then, reluctantly, I nodded. "All right, I promise. Now let's have it."

Immediately, the tension between us cleared. He lit a cigar, as usual. And, as usual, arched the still-smoldering match into my wastebasket. As I pointedly moved my ashtray closer to him, he leaned back in his chair, blew a smoke ring up toward the ceiling and began to talk: "Biggs's mother, as far as I can judge, was pretty much of a tramp all her life. However, unlike some women, she apparently figured out that she was better off selling it, instead of giving it away. Or, at least, she got smart enough to trade it for a few worldly goods. But it apparently took her a while to get the message. For a long time, when she was young, she stashed Biggs in a series of foster homes while she flopped from one guy to another. Her husband, Biggs's father, was a teen-aged sailor. He took off before the kid was born. They lived in St. Louis, if I remember correctly. Anyhow, Nancy Biggs came to San Francisco about fifteen years ago—with the boy, who'd've been four years old at the time. Like I say, by the time she got to San Francisco, she was getting smarter. She also got lucky and married a guy named Kress, who was a prosperous cement contractor. That lasted six years, I think. Then she married Chester Frazer, who owns three good-size supermarkets. Chester's not much to look at. He's old and kind of shriveled. In fact, when I was interrogating him in connection with Nancy's death, it came out that he was impotent during most of his marriage—a condition that Nancy, apparently, did everything in her power to aggravate, instead of the other way around. I get the feeling that she used Frazer's impotence like a club. And, meanwhile, she could play around all she wanted. For her, I guess, it was an ideal setup. What's better for a tramp than an impotent husband? And a well-off impotent husband at that?"

"How old was she when she died?"

"Thirty-nine. And Frazer was fifty-six, if I remember right. But he looked seventy. They'd been married for almost eight years—eight long, hard years. I gather that the six years before she got wounded were almost worse than the two years since."

"What about James Biggs?"

"Apparently he was always screwed up. I don't know much about him before his mother married Frazer because Frazer is my main source of information concerning the kid. James was about eleven when Nancy and Frazer got married. Already, he had a juvenile file that looked like a con's. If he'd been a slum kid, he'd've been locked up, no question. As it was, Biggs started getting into some pretty heavy scrapes. Once he apparently got pissed off because some kids wouldn't let him into their club. So he proceeded to pile some kerosene-soaked rags against the door of the clubhouse and set them on fire. Another

time he took a piece of iron pipe to a kid and just about killed
the kid. Then there were the little girls. There's nothing about
the girls in his file, but Frazer intimated that Biggs had a lot of
real kinky ways with the little girls. So, after a couple of years
of this, Frazer had enough. He sent Biggs to a place called the
Long Valley School. It's a place for incorrigible boys, up in
Lake County. But Biggs was an incorrigible's incorrigible.
How he lasted four years, I'll never understand. But he did,
thanks to Frazer's money, I gather."

"What kind of things did he do?"

"Well, first, he took up homosexuality. Which in a place like
that isn't uncommon, of course. But he added a new wrinkle.
He decided that he needed some extra spending money. So
he kept his eyes open and spotted a couple of male teachers who had a thing going with some of the students. Which
isn't uncommon, either. In the meantime, Biggs had become
an electronics genius. I forgot to mention that. So he wired the
two teachers' rooms for sound and proceeded to shake them
down for fifty bucks or so every month. With the money, I understand, he bought more electronics equipment. He also
cornered the drug concession at the Long Valley School. But,
of course, that wasn't until his senior year."

"So he graduated. Then what?"

"Well, then he went to San Jose State College, if you can
believe that. Except that he only lasted a year—and a very
shaky year, at that. It seems that he developed an interest in
the opposite sex. Which is to say that he was interested in both
sexes. But, anyhow, it was his interest in the opposite sex that
got him bounced out of San Jose State in the middle of his
second term—and bounced out hard. It was something about
half strangling a girl in the process of trying to make love to
her—or to rape her, more like it. The girl's parents decided not
to sign a complaint."

"They'd rather let him try it again on someone else."

"Naturally. It's the American way. So, anyhow, Biggs came
back to San Francisco and spent the next few months lying
around the house, as I remember. There were a lot of pretty
freaky breaking-and-entering squeals that broke out in the
neighborhood about that time, and a couple of women got

pretty badly scared. But nobody could ever pin anything on Biggs, even though the morals squad, for one, gave it a pretty good try. So then Nancy Frazer got shot, as we all know, almost two years ago. According to what Frazer said, the shock of her injury seemed—on the surface, anyhow—to change Biggs. At least he spent a lot of time with his dear old mom, bringing her juice and medicine."

"A lethal dose."

"That came later, maybe. At first, though, he was quite dutiful. Maybe, right from the first, he figured that he'd be better off with her dead and was trying to work out an angle. Maybe not. Whichever it was, he hung around the house a lot, helping out. Then he started to drink with old Mom. And, Frazer claims, the two of them started taking drugs—which, apparently, Biggs had no trouble getting. Frazer thinks Mom supplied the money, and Biggs got the stuff. Frazer isn't sure. He *is* sure, though, that a lot of money went from him to Nancy, who had no way of spending it, except to give it to Biggs. A psychiatrist who examined Biggs for us, surreptitiously, said that Biggs was probably in love with his mother. You know, the old Oedipus skam. Maybe the psychiatrist was right. If he *was* right, it would account for Biggs's solicitous behavior. Personally, I don't buy it. But then, I'm not a great fan of the psychiatrist."

"If the psychiatrist was right, though, it might account for Biggs harassing me—and Ann. He's after me for causing his mother's death. And he's after Ann for revenge. I killed his lover, so he'll kill mine."

Friedman snorted. "A minute ago, you were saying that Biggs killed her."

"Maybe he did, consciously or unconsciously. Maybe he's blocked it out. And going after me would help him block it out even more."

Friedman grimaced, "You're really into this psychological crap, aren't you? That's what comes of cops with college educations, I suppose."

"What happened after she died? Where did Biggs go?"

"He didn't go anywhere. Frazer went—got out of the house

and left it to Biggs. I got the impression that Frazer couldn't wait to get out and breathe some fresh air."

"Is Biggs still in the house?"

Friedman eyed me warily, mutely reminding me of my promise. "He's still there," he answered. "Frazer offered to let him stay as long as he wanted, rent-free. He—"

My phone rang. As I lifted the receiver, Friedman whispered that he'd see me in the morning, then airily waved his cigar in a gesture of good-bye. I watched an inch-long cigar ash fall slow-motion to the floor.

"There's a Mrs. Carstairs to see you, Lieutenant. Mrs. Grace Carstairs." It was the receptionist.

Surprised, I grunted. "Send her in." I walked to my door and opened it, watching a tall, rangy woman striding toward me. She was dressed for a funeral in an expensively cut dark flannel coat and dark hat. Her face was long and angular, with widely spaced eyes and a large, unattractive mouth. She moved with the loose, confident assurance of the privileged class. Watching her, I experienced a momentary pang of painful recall. My ex-wife had moved like that. But my wife had been beautiful. A beautiful, tawny predator.

"Are you Lieutenant Hastings?" Her voice, too, evoked an aura of privilege. I waywardly wondered whether she'd gone to Bryn Mawr, like my wife. The broad, deceptively lazy accent was the same.

"Yes," I answered. "I'm Lieutenant Hastings. Come in, please." As I ushered her into the office, I frowned at my own deference. She was, after all, a suspect in a murder case. Just another suspect.

I gestured to the visitor's armchair, but she chose a side chair. She crossed her legs, arranging herself in a forward-leaning, slant-shouldered posture. She sat with her large, bony hands clasped, one elbow resting on her crossed thigh. A few inches above the floor, her alligator pump twitched as she talked. "I've come to ask what it is that you want, Lieutenant. I'd appreciate it if you'd tell me."

"I want to find out who murdered your mother."

Her unattractive mouth twisted derisively. "It seems to me

that you're looking in the wrong places. No wonder you haven't found him yet."

"How do you mean, 'the wrong places'?"

"I gather that you're questioning my brother and my husband."

"Among others." I paused, then said, "We have to question you, too, Mrs. Carstairs. Is that why you're here?"

"I'm here," she said, "because I simply won't have policemen hanging around my house. I simply won't *have* it." As she spoke, her voice rose to a higher, shriller note. Her clasped hands, I saw, were knuckle-white.

"I wish it weren't necessary to question either you or your husband, Mrs. Carstairs. We—"

"There's a—a detective at my house right this very moment," she protested. "I just called home, from the funeral parlor. And Charles said that someone named Canelli had just come. He wants to question my *daughters.*"

I nodded. "That's right. He's acting on my orders."

"But *why,* for God's sake?" Momentarily, her voice broke. Suddenly defeated, she slumped back in her chair, blinking back tears.

Speaking gently, I explained to her that it was my duty to investigate anyone who could have gained by the death of her mother. Then tentatively I asked her to account for her time last night.

Blinking with blank, baffled bemusement, she slowly shook her head. "I can't believe this. I *simply* can't believe it."

Deciding not to reply, I waited. Finally she asked, "Does this concern Charles? Or me?"

"It's just that I've got to get all the facts together, Mrs. Carstairs. We don't suspect either one of you. But you could have information that we need—information that you might not even know is important."

She bit her lip, twisted her white-knuckled hands and muttered, "You've spoken to Charles about last night, I gather."

I didn't respond.

"He said that you did." She said it accusingly, as if she'd caught me trying to trick her.

Still without speaking, I decided to nod.

"I suppose that your—your suspicions are aroused because we left the party separately. Is that it?"

"It's not a question of suspicions, Mrs. Carstairs. I've already told you that. It's a question of assembling the facts. That's my job. If I don't do it, somebody else will. It's as simple as that." As I spoke, I glanced pointedly at the clock. It was already six-thirty. I was anxious to see Ann.

"Well—" As she drew a long, reluctant breath, her eyes fell. "There's nothing so unusual, you know, about two people leaving a party separately."

"I know."

"We—" She hesitated, then continued defensively, "We had a—a little misunderstanding. It was nothing serious. And, besides, Charles was tired. He wanted to leave, and I wanted to stay. So finally he just took the car and left."

"What time did he leave?"

"About ten-thirty, I think."

I nodded. Her story checked with Canelli's information. "What time did you leave, Mrs. Carstairs?"

"I left about an hour later. Maybe an hour and a half. It was before midnight, anyhow."

"How'd you get home?"

"A friend loaned me her car. Both she and her husband had driven to the party separately. She insisted that I take it."

"Where was the party, Mrs. Carstairs?"

"At the San Francisco Art Museum. Actually, it was a buffet for the opening of the Chagall exhibit."

The museum formed one point of a triangle joining her own home in Pacific Heights to her mother's home, in Sea Cliff. At midnight, she could have reached Sea Cliff in ten minutes from the museum. Another ten minutes would have taken her home from Sea Cliff.

I decided not to press her further. She was again showing unmistakable signs of distress, and I needed her cooperation more than I needed additional information. I took a few minutes to double-check Carstairs' story, then dismissed her. As I watched her leaving, I was wondering what Canelli would find out from the Carstairs children.

Twelve

I parked around the corner from Ann's building and walked. Midway in the block, I saw Galton and his partner, parked in their cruiser. Exchanging a few surreptitious words with Galton, I learned that everything was normal. I told him that I'd arranged for his replacement and said goodnight.

Dan Haywood, Ann's older son, opened the door. At sixteen, he was a handsome boy with his mother's thick ash-blond hair and clear gray eyes. He'd been slow to accept me as his mother's lover, but now we were at ease with each other, perhaps soon to become friends.

"Did you find the creep?" he asked in a low voice.

I shook my head. He sighed, shook his head and gestured to the living room. "She's in there, Frank. I'm doing my geometry. We've got a test tomorrow."

"Good luck."

"Thanks. See you later."

Ann was waiting for me in the doorway of the living room. She'd changed into a pair of old corduroy slacks and a sweater. With her hair hanging loose, arms straight at her sides and chin slightly tucked, she looked like a chastened child. She was wearing the woolly slippers I'd given her for Christmas.

Without speaking, I circled her waist with both arms and drew her close. With her arms around my neck, she returned the embrace, fitting her body almost fiercely to mine. We stood swaying in urgent embrace, exchanging the small, secret movements of love. Finally I drew a deep breath, stepped back and pushed her out to arm's length. "Is that lust," I said, "or nerves?"

She smiled. "If you have to ask, the message wasn't getting through."

I drew her to the sofa, and we sat down close together. "Where's Billy?" I asked.

"In the back room watching TV."

"Was he scared when he came home and saw your room?"

"No. He was excited—and a little disappointed that you weren't here."

"Did you tell him that I had to leave?"

She nodded.

We sat silently for a moment, touching each other. Finally she said quietly, "Are the two things connected—what happened last night and this afternoon?" Asking the question, she looked straight ahead. Her hand in mine tightened almost imperceptibly.

"I'm not sure. But I think so."

"Are there two of them?"

"In a way."

"Aren't you going to tell me what it's all about, Frank?"

I'd already decided that, if she asked, I'd tell her. The story took almost a half-hour to tell. When I'd finished, she pressed my hand.

"It's a terrible story," she said. "I'm frightened."

"He's only one person, Ann. A teen-ager."

"So was Billy the Kid."

Caught off guard, I suddenly guffawed. She turned to look at me with a slow, solemn stare—which only aggravated my perverse amusement. I saw the line of her small jaw stubbornly shift.

"I'm sorry," I said finally. "But Biggs is so—so completely different from Billy the Kid that—" Shaking my head, I broke off, still chuckling.

"Billy the Kid was a homicidal maniac," she said primly.

"I know. I'm sorry."

Still holding my hand, she squeezed. "Sometimes," she said slowly, "I wonder why men become policemen."

"Sometimes I wonder, too."

"It must be something to do with the—the excitement of the chase."

I shook my head. "I don't know. I've thought about it, but I don't know. There isn't much excitement, though. And not much chasing. Mostly it's just a slow, plodding exercise in futility."

"But it's dangerous. Last night, you could have . . ." She broke off, shaking her head. Again I felt her hand tighten in mine.

"Listen, Ann, we weren't in any real danger last night. And you weren't in any danger today. If you'd been in the house, he wouldn't've come inside. He wasn't after you. He was after your—your pillow."

"But he's sick. And he could be working himself up to something."

I didn't reply—didn't look at her. Because she was right.

"What're you going to do about him, Frank?"

"I'm going to have a little talk with him. Tomorrow." I hadn't told her that I'd been forbidden access to Biggs. To change the subject I said, "Is the cabin at Stinson Beach all set for the weekend?"

"Yes. I talked to Marcie today at school. Do you think you can go?"

"I'm planning on it."

She twisted to face me fully. Her gray eyes sought somberly to hold mine as she said, "Be careful, darling. Be careful of him."

I smiled at her and slipped my arm around her shoulders. "Just keep thinking of him as Billy the Kid," I said, teasing her. "And think of me as Sheriff Pat Garrett."

Thirteen

"What about the Carstairs' daughters?" I asked Canelli. "Could you find out anything last night?"

Canelli set his coffee cup carefully on the corner of my desk, using a folded piece of paper as a coaster. "I didn't find out too much about the night of the murder," he answered. "One kid didn't hear a thing. The other kid—the oldest one—heard someone come home late at night, but she didn't know what time it was. Like she said, she just opened one eye and then went back to sleep. But I picked up a little something else. One of the kids—the youngest one—let it drop that her mother and father've been arguing a lot. Which maybe isn't news. But then it turns out that they were arguing about money. Because, the kid says, Carstairs is in way over his head on some real-estate deal. He's really sweating."

"Nice kid," Culligan said sourly.

"It wasn't quite like that," Canelli protested mildly. "I mean, if I do say so, it took a little working her around. She didn't just start unloading, or anything."

"Canelli has a way with children and dogs," Friedman observed. "Right, Canelli?"

Canelli tentatively smiled at his superior officer.

"Anything else?" I asked.

"One thing, maybe," Canelli answered. "See, Mrs. Carstairs wasn't exactly what you'd call cooperative when she came home from seeing you. She wouldn't even talk to me. She got home about seven o'clock, I guess. And right away Carstairs went out. Where, he didn't say. But they just said a couple of words to each other, and then Carstairs left. I had the feeling they were sore at each other, or something. That's really how I got to talk to the girls, see. I mean, Carstairs was out, and Mrs. Carstairs right away got on the phone as soon as she got home, arranging for the funeral, and everything. So the kids and me, we sat in the kitchen. They're all turned on, you might say, about the murder, and who did it, and everything. They were asking me how we were going to solve it, and who we suspected. And—"

"Canelli. Please." Friedman held up a traffic-stopping palm. "Never mind the build-up. What's the 'one thing'?"

"Well, I was just going to say that the youngest one—the same one who told me about her father's problems—she asked me about the chauffeur. Fry. She said that she heard her mother talking on the phone about the chauffeur, and how he saw whoever did it."

"She was probably talking to her brother," I said thoughtfully. "That's good. Maybe the pot's starting to stew."

"That's what I thought, Lieutenant. But what interested me was how the kid said that the mother sounded real worried, talking about what Fry saw."

"Kids have big imaginations," Friedman observed. "And it sounds like this kid's could be bigger than usual."

"I know," Canelli admitted. "I thought about it. I mean, this kid is always talking. Always thinking, too. You can tell that. She's got these big, sparkling eyes, and you only have to look at her to know she's real smart. Still—" He shrugged. "To me, she sounded like she's telling a straight story."

"How old is this kid?" Culligan asked.

"She's eleven."

"Eleven-year-old kids like to dramatize," Friedman said. "That's in addition to their oversize imaginations."

"What about the lab?" I asked Canelli. "Did you check with them last night?"

"Oh, yeah, Lieutenant, I sure did. They said that, first thing this morning, they'd have a full report for you. But, just talking to them, it didn't sound like they had much."

"What about the traceability of the Kleen-Eeze?"

"Well, they're always pretty cagey, you know, down there. They said that it would depend on a lot of variables, and everything. But I got the feeling that the oil and Kleen-Eeze mixture was pretty tenacious, as they call it."

"Whether it's tenacious or not," Friedman observed, "you could still use it to get the pot stewing. If the murderer thinks we could vacuum some Kleen-Eeze out of his carpet and make him for murder, he might start to sweat. Especially if he'd stated he hadn't been in the Gaines's garage."

"Did you ask the Carstairs whether they'd been in the Gaines's garage in the last two days?" I asked Canelli.

"Yessir. And they hadn't. Either one of them."

"Jonathan hasn't, either," I said thoughtfully.

"Maybe you should start sending the vacuum-cleaner crew around," Friedman suggested. "It couldn't hurt."

"We couldn't vacuum the Carstairs place without a court order."

"So get a court order. Do you want me to get one?"

I shook my head. "Let's do a little checking first."

Friedman shrugged.

I turned to Culligan. "Why don't you and Sigler start checking Carstairs out? Let's find out about his financial status and the status of that real-estate deal. Don't make a whole lot of noise about it, but don't try to keep it too quiet, either. Maybe Carstairs will start to sweat. Then, if you have time, do the same thing for Jonathan Esterbrook. For all we know, he could be down to his last ten dollars. Meanwhile, Canelli and I will make the rounds again, starting at the Gaines house. Let's see whether anything's changed overnight."

"Suits me." Culligan got to his feet and slouched out of the office. I told Canelli to get the car and wait for me in front of the Hall. When Canelli had gone I asked Pete whether he'd heard anything relating to Biggs.

"Not yet," he answered. "But it's only nine-thirty in the morning. We'll hear, believe me." He hesitated, then obliquely asked, "What'd you do last night?"

"I stopped by Ann's for an hour or so, then went home."

He nodded gravely. "Good."

"I only promised to stay away from Biggs last night," I reminded him.

He nodded again. "Now, I'd like you to extend the promise until I can see what the brass says."

For a long, taut moment we mutely tested each other's resolution. Finally, breaking off the staring contest, I stood up, jerked open my desk drawer and took out my revolver.

"I'll see you later, then," I said abruptly. "Or at least I'll call you." I looked down at him, so complacently comfortable, lolling belly-up in my visitor's chair. "Lock the door behind you."

His full lips moved in a secret, subtle smile. "Don't I always?"

As we pulled up in front of the Gaines house Canelli looked up and down the block. "Isn't there a black-and-white car on duty?" he asked, surprised.

"One day is enough," I answered, swinging the door open and getting out of the car.

"Yeah, I see what you mean."

As he pressed the doorbell I said, "Let's split up. You poke around the garage and the garden—and that gardener's building in back of the garage, too, where Fry seems to hang out. Maybe you can turn up something."

"How about the alley?"

I shrugged. "Suit yourself."

The door opened, revealing Charlotte Young. Today she was dressed in a stiffly starched blouse and blue skirt. Beneath the short sleeves of the blouse, her biceps were muscular as a man's. "Hello, Lieutenant." She stood stolidly blocking the doorway, surveying me with cool, calm inquiry.

"Is Mr. Gaines at home?" I asked.

She nodded. "He's in the kitchen, having breakfast."

"Thanks." As I stepped forward, she reluctantly gave way, backing into the hallway. Canelli moved around me, making for the back of the house. Charlotte Young closed the front door, then stood against the hallway wall, impassively facing me.

"I don't think Mr. Gaines will be very happy to see you," she said.

"Why's that?"

"Because he's all shook up, that's why."

"Is he grief-stricken? Is that what you're saying?"

Her full lips parted in an ironically mocking smile. "No, that's not what I'm saying, Lieutenant. I'm saying that his hands shake whenever he lights a cigarette."

"Why's that?"

She lifted her chunky shoulders. "Might be you've got him a little worried. Who knows?"

I stepped into the living room, beckoning for her to follow me. Lowering my voice, I said, "Don't play games with me, Miss Young. If you know something about Gaines and the murder, tell me."

"I don't *know* a thing." Her voice, too, was lowered. Plainly enjoying herself, she waited for me to continue probing.

"You suspect something, then. What is it?"

"I suspect," she said slowly, "that something is going on around here, that's all. Last night, Peter got a little more swacked than usual. And about eleven o'clock I heard him leave his room and stumble downstairs. So since I'm going to be an officer of the court someday, like you said, I thought I should see what's happening. So I followed him downstairs. And come to find out old Peter was going into the living room, where the master of the house was sitting, listening to Mantovani or someone on the record player. I didn't hear what was said, because of the Mantovani, but pretty soon Peter comes stumbling back. I was in the kitchen, pretending to make myself some soup. I saw him coming along the hallway, mumbling and nodding and smiling to himself, like he'd just found money on the sidewalk or something. He didn't see me. He just went stumbling along up the stairs. So then, just when I decide I may as well quit stirring the soup and go to bed, here comes Rupert. And Rupert was looking like he'd swallowed a pickle sideways, as they used to say in my neighborhood."

"What happened then?"

"Rupert went outside and got in his car, which was in the driveway. And he drove away. So I poured the soup down the sink and went to bed." She rotated her strong, squared-off hands, turning the pink palms upward. "End of report."

"When did Rupert get home?"

"About midnight. Maybe a little sooner. He wasn't out long."

"Where'd he go, do you know?"

She shook her head.

"What'd he do when he got home?"

"He went to bed. I didn't see him. But I heard him."

"What about Peter Fry?"

"He stayed in bed. Everything was cool."

"Where's Peter Fry now?"

"He's in the garage."

Nodding my thanks, I walked down the hallway that led both to the back doors and the kitchen. As I passed the open door of the kitchen, I glanced inside. Rupert Gaines sat at a breakfast counter, bowed over a coffee cup. Smoke from a smoldering cigarette curved in thick, slow tendrils around his head. He didn't raise his head, didn't see me. Charlotte Young came down the hallway behind me. As I opened the door leading through the covered passageway to the garage, I spoke softly to her. "I don't want Mr. Gaines to leave the house until I've talked to him. Do you understand?"

Smiling with knowing malice, she nodded.

I found Peter Fry using a stiff-bristled pushbroom to clean the floor of the garage. Except for his shoes, he was dressed as he'd been the day before. Bent over the broom, his face was flushed and florid—a drinker's face, after a hard night. As I glanced at the spot where Mrs. Gaines had fallen, Fry sensed my presence, quickly turning toward me. He followed my gaze toward the spot between the Cadillac's front fender and the wall. The floor was only slightly oil-stained.

"Kleen-Eeze is great stuff," he said quietly, leaning on the broom's handle and regarding me quizzically.

I'd already decided how I wanted to approach him. Tersely, without embellishments, I repeated what Charlotte Young had told me, then waited for his response.

He didn't reply immediately, but instead simply stood leaning on his broom, staring at me with his watery, half-focused eyes. His thin body was slack inside his clothes. Not yet fifty, Peter Fry was a burnt-out case.

"What did you and Gaines talk about last night?" I pressed.

The tortured lines of his face shifted into an expression of wry, exhausted humor. As he smiled, his eyes seemed to sink deep beneath the antic tufts of his ginger eyebrows.

"We talked about life and death, Lieutenant."

"Be a little more specific, Fry. And be a little more concise, too. I've got a busy day."

"Ah—" He bobbed his head, elaborately nodding. "You're going to spring the trap today, is that it?"

"That could depend on you."

"Exactly." He raised a pleased, professorial forefinger. "That's exactly what I was telling Mr. Gaines, as a matter of fact. It could all depend on me. Do you have any experience with autohypnosis, Lieutenant?"

"I can't say that I do. Why?"

"Because sometimes when I've, ah, had a few drinks, it seems to me as if I can put myself back into almost any experience I please. I suppose, really, it's nothing very remarkable. Maybe it's just daydreaming with a purpose, for all I know. But, in any case, I suddenly had the feeling, last night, that I could relive those fateful moments in the alley, night before last. And it occurred to me that I should tell someone about it."

"If you're going to tell anyone, Fry, tell me. Now."

"Ah, but I *am* telling you. That's the whole point, you see. I've decided to assume the role of detective's helper."

"Did you tell Gaines last night that you recognized the murderer?"

"I strongly suggested it, let's say."

"What was his reaction?"

"Shock, I'd say."

"That's all?"

"That's all. Almost immediately, however, he ordered me to my room. My stepfather, as a matter of fact, used the same tone with me. And I remember that—"

"Yesterday," I said, "you denied that you could recognize the figure you saw running away."

He broadly winked at me, mockingly crafty. "That was yesterday, Lieutenant. Today, it's a different game."

"It looks to me," I said slowly, "like a game of blackmail. Which happens to be illegal—and very dangerous, too."

"We live in a hostile world, Lieutenant. Danger is everywhere. As who should know better than I."

"Does Gaines think you suspect him—that you can identify him? Is that what you're telling me?"

"Ah, no. There's the artistry, you see. I merely suggested that I could perhaps identify someone. Between you and me—" He winked again. "Between you and me, it could be anyone. As I said, I was being a detective's helper."

"But why, for God's sake?"

Still propped against his broom handle, he lifted his bony shoulders. "It seemed like a good idea. It seemed like a wonderful idea, in fact. After all, my future is uncertain. I have to make provisions. My inheritance won't take me very far."

"I don't think you'd be very successful as a blackmailer, Fry. You're not tough enough."

"I might not be very tough, that's true. But I'm desperate, Lieutenant. In fact, I'm scared silly."

We stood in the chill of the garage, silently gazing at each other. What Fry had done, I realized, was to confirm the fiction I'd contrived yesterday, when I'd said that he could identify the murderer. Fry was doing my work for me. And Gaines, perhaps, had taken the bait.

I left Fry where he stood, and reentered the house through the passageway. I found Gaines still in the kitchen, sitting slumped over his empty coffee cup. Without preamble, I asked him bluntly whether he believed Fry could identify the murderer.

As if he hadn't understood, Gaines turned to stare at me with blank, baffled eyes. His pale, beard-stubbled face was drawn, his frail neck corded with fatigue and tension. His poet's good looks weren't surviving the strain.

"Did you talk to Fry last night?" I asked him.

"Y—" He painfully swallowed. "Yes, for a little while. Just a few minutes, really."

"And did he tell you at that time that he could identify your wife's murderer—that, in fact, he'd recognized the murderer, running away?"

"He—" The tip of his tongue circled pale, uncertain lips. "He said something about it. But I—I didn't listen. He was drunk, and I told him to go to bed. He—he knows better than to get drunk like that and bother us. Flora told him that the next time it happened, she'd—" He suddenly broke off. His dark, opaque eyes sought the bottom of his coffee cup.

"What did you do, Mr. Gaines, after you ordered Fry to go to bed?"

"I—I went out. I needed some cigarettes."

"Did you have to go far for your cigarettes?"

As if the question alarmed him, he anxiously raised his eyes. Then he quickly shook his head. "No, not far. But I—I took a little drive. I knew I'd have trouble sleeping. So I drove down the Great Highway, along the beach."

"What time did you get back? Do you remember?"

"Why, it—it must've been midnight, I guess. I—I don't know. I remember, though, that the house was dark."

"You didn't see anyone last night while you were driving?"

"No one."

"Did you call anyone?"

His dark brows twitched together in a puzzled frown. "Call anyone?"

"Yes. Susan Platt, for instance. Did you call her?"

The frown was no longer puzzled. Horrified comprehension tore at his face like fingers ripping at an actor's rubber mask.

"Wh—why would I call Susan?" he whispered. "It was too—too late to call anyone. It was almost midnight. I *told* you that."

"Do you think she would have minded?" I asked quietly. "Seeing that you're such good friends?"

"I d—don't know what y—you mean." With an obvious

effort, he summoned an expression of tortured outrage. "What *do* you mean, anyhow?"

"I mean that, yesterday, I had a long talk with Susan Platt. Didn't she tell you?"

"Well, sh—she said that, yes, you'd talked to her. But I— I—" He began to shake his head slowly, doggedly. "But that doesn't mean that—"

"She told me that you were lovers, Mr. Gaines. Was she telling me a lie?"

"A—a lie?"

"*Are* you lovers?"

"Lovers?"

"That's the question, Mr. Gaines. Are you going to give me an answer?"

Suddenly his head snapped up, his eyes blazed. His voice cracked as it slipped into a high, petulant falsetto. "No, I'm *not* going to give you an answer, Lieutenant. I—I'm going to call my lawyer. This time, I'm really going to call him. And I—I'm not going to say anything more to you. Not another word." The stool toppled over as he planted his feet firmly on the floor, facing me furiously. His face was flushed, his throat worked convulsively. It was the same performance he'd given yesterday.

"Not another word," he shrilled, then turned toward the door.

Thoughtfully, I watched him flounce down the hallway, his hips swinging viciously. Almost everyone, I was thinking, discounted Gaines as a lightweight, incapable of murder. I wondered whether they were right.

Fourteen

"Where to, Lieutenant?" Canelli vigorously slammed his door.

"I think I'm going to drop you off at the Carstairs'. I've got something else to do."

"Right." He started the engine and pulled away from the curb. "What'd Gaines tell you?"

"He said he was going to call his lawyer."

"I'll bet that's what Carstairs is going to tell me, too."

"Probably. Did you turn up anything at the Gaines house?" I asked.

"Naw. But then, I didn't know what I was looking for."

I smiled wearily. "Who does, Canelli? If we knew what we were looking for, we wouldn't be looking."

"Hey, Lieutenant, that's pretty good." He nodded over the steering wheel, pleased. "I hope I can remember that."

"I probably heard it from Lieutenant Friedman."

"Yeah, it sounds a little like him. He's really a smart man. I mean, he kind of reminds me of a spider, or something, sitting in the middle of his web, with his fingers on everything. He just sits and thinks. You know?"

I nodded. "I know."

"I heard somewhere that Lieutenant Friedman started out to be a rabbi. Is that right?"

"That's not the half of it, Canelli. He started out to be a

rabbi, but then he changed his mind and decided that he wanted to be an actor."

The car swerved slightly as Canelli stared at me, amazed. "You're *kidding*."

I shook my head. "I'm not kidding."

"*An actor?*"

"That's right. In Hollywood. He was in several movies, too. All bit parts. In those days, he says, he was slim and handsome. But all the time he had to support himself as a fry cook. So finally he chucked it and decided that he needed a civil service job."

"Jeeze, I can't believe it." Marveling, Canelli shook his head as we drove two blocks in silence. Then he said, "It's interesting, you know. I mean, when you think about it, both you and Lieutenant Friedman had other careers and everything before you joined the force."

I snorted, at the same time gesturing for him to turn right. We were within three blocks of the Carstairs house. "I'm afraid neither one of us were very big successes, though."

"Jeeze, I wouldn't say that, Lieutenant. I mean, you were a professional football player. That's a whole lot."

"A second-string professional football player," I answered ruefully. "And then a second-string publicity man, working for my father-in-law. I'd've been better off as a fry cook and bit player."

Canelli's frown was sympathetic. "Your wife was real rich. Is that it?"

"That's it, Canelli. Real rich. Don't ever marry a rich girl." I pointed ahead. "Pull over there. If anything comes up, you can contact me through Communications. Otherwise, I'll see you at the Hall about five o'clock. Right?"

He nodded decisively. "Right. And good luck, Lieutenant."

"Thanks, Canelli. It's possible I might need it."

I'd already gotten Biggs's address from the files. The house was in the Sunset district of the city, five miles from the Carstairs apartment in Pacific Heights. I drove slowly, enjoying the warm spring sunshine. The Sunset was a middle-class neighborhood—long lines of stucco row houses sloping monotonously down to the ocean beach. Biggs's house, actually Chester Frazer's, was more elaborate than the other houses in the block—two stories instead of one, with imitation hand-hewn beams and imitation red Spanish tile accenting the gleaming white stucco. A scrawny, spiky palm tree grew in front of the house.

I drove past, cruising slowly. A red Dodge Dart was parked in the driveway. Yellowed newspapers and rotting circulars littered the low-growing ivy of the small front garden. The entryway, too, was paper-strewn. I continued on around the corner and stopped at the closest call box, three blocks away. A moment later I was talking to Friedman.

"Where are you?" he asked.

"I'm on Forty-third Avenue and Taraval," I answered evenly.

There was a brief moment of silence. Then: "Near the Frazer place."

"Yes."

Another silence before he said finally, "I've just come from the captain's office."

He didn't have to finish it. From the tone of his voice, I knew that nothing had changed. Matching his short, terse silence, I also matched the impersonal note in his voice as I said, "I dropped Canelli at the Carstairs place. Will you get Sigler, or someone, to join up with him? I want him to go to Jonathan Esterbrook's, too. Then I'll have a meeting at five o'clock."

"Will do."

"Is there anything from the lab?" Asking the question, I realized that I was speaking to him as I might to a stranger.

"They've given us a negative on everything," he replied. "No blood spots on Fry's clothing, or Gaines's clothing, either. Same for Charlotte Young's things. Fry and Gaines had traces of Kleen-Eeze on their shoes, which is normal. No prints on either the weapon or the purse. Almost certainly, the murderer used surgical gloves. And according to Charlotte Young's statement to the lab crew, no one's shoes or clothes are missing from the Gaines house." He paused, then said, "I think we should be making the same tests on Jonathan Esterbrook and Carstairs. I don't see why you're holding back."

"If we come down too heavily on the Carstairs," I answered stiffly, "we'll lose their cooperation."

"Such as it is."

"It's better than nothing. And as far as Jonathan is concerned, we'd have no way of knowing whether he'd ditched his clothing."

"There's still the possibility of vacuuming his rugs."

"Let's talk about it at five o'clock tonight."

"All right."

We endured another long, awkward moment of silence, then broke the connection. I drove directly to the Frazer house, parking three doors away. As I walked back to the house, I glanced up and down the block. Was it possible, I wondered, that Captain Kreiger had secretly ordered the house staked out?

I kicked a scattering of circulars from underfoot and rang the bell. Hearing the soft sound of approaching footsteps, I unconsciously unbuttoned my jacket and raised my hand to my waist, ready to draw my revolver. A chain rattled and a lock clicked. The door opened, revealing James Biggs.

Wearing sneakers, blue jeans and a sweatshirt, he looked like countless other teen-agers. His features were regular, his dark-blond hair trimmed earlobe-long. His face was strangely pale, but well-shaped.

Only the eyes were different. The eyes, and the mouth.

His eyes were fixed—bright blue button-eyes, shining with manic intensity. His mouth was incredibly mobile—constantly twitching, even when he was silent. When he talked, his lips writhed and twisted and sneered, giving a surreal, sinister emphasis to his words.

"Hello, Lieutenant Hastings." He moved back, waving me inside with an elaborate sweep of his arm. "Come in. I've been expecting you."

"I'll bet you have." I stepped inside, closed the door behind me and gestured for him to go first. The gesture amused him. Almost gaily he turned and strode into the living room. He went immediately to a small portable bar.

Aftershock

"How about a drink, Lieutenant? What would you like? Whiskey? Wine? Coca-Cola?" He was almost capering for me, playing the antic host.

"Nothing, thanks." I glanced deliberately around the room. Everywhere I looked, I saw evidence of neglect and decay. Dried bits of food were everywhere, on and off the crusted plates. Cigarette butts overflowed the ashtrays and protruded from the rotting bits of leftover food. Magazines and newspapers littered every chair. Although the window shades were drawn, slivers of the bright afternoon sunlight slanted into the room. Countless dust particles, disturbed by our movements, clouded the narrow yellow shafts of light.

He eyed the bottles behind the bar, finally selecting one and filling a dirty glass. "I think I'll have some Chablis." He took the glass of wine to a nearby easy chair, where he perched on the arm. "It's a little early for anything heavier, don't you think?"

"I wouldn't know. I don't drink."

He sipped the wine, eyeing me over the edge of the glass. "But you *used* to drink, didn't you, Lieutenant? You used to drink quite a lot."

I tried to keep my eyes steady, my expression inscrutable. How had he known? How much more did he know?

"In fact," he continued airily, waving his glass of Chablis, "I understand that, when you first became a policeman, you almost drank yourself out of a job."

"I didn't come here to talk about myself, Biggs. I came to talk about you—and to warn you to keep away from Mrs. Haywood."

"Ah—" He nodded, sipped the wine and set the half-filled glass aside. "Ah, so that's it."

"That's it."

"Is this an official visit, then?"

"No," I answered slowly, still struggling to meet the unnatural brightness of his eyes. "No, this isn't an official visit. This is a personal warning—from me to you."

"Ah, good." He slid off the arm, collapsing at his ease in the comfortable chair. "Then we can talk freely. Is that it?"

"That's it."

"Who should start?" It was a coy, rapt question. "You, or me?"

"You make it sound like a parlor game."

He airily waved his hand. "Life is a game, Lieutenant. To win, you have to take risks. You, for instance. You're taking a risk right now—right this moment. Isn't that true?"

"You seem to know a lot about my business, Biggs."

He nodded. "Yes, I do. But it shouldn't surprise you, Lieutenant. My whole life, you might say, is twisted around yours, and vice versa. You killed my mother. If I don't do something, you could kill me, too. So I've got to protect myself. You can see that, can't you?" He spoke with elaborately stylized patience, as if he were trying to explain a difficult point to a backward child. But, in contradiction, his blue button-eyes hardened. The bogus, brittle-bright gaiety was suddenly gone. Ostensibly relaxed in the easy chair, his body was actually coiled tight.

"I didn't kill your mother, Biggs. If anyone killed her, it was you. We both know it."

"Now, surely, Lieutenant, you don't expect me to admit that, do you?" As he said it, he blinked at me, batting his eyes. It was a playful, perverse invitation. He was mutely admitting that, yes, he'd killed her—but that he defied me to prove it.

He was toying with me—expertly playing some sly, cynical game.

Friedman had been right about him. Again, Friedman had been right.

"No," I answered slowly, "I don't expect you to admit it. But I'm sure that you either killed her or made it possible for her to die. I think that, at the least, you waited for her to drink enough alcohol, and then let her have enough barbiturates to kill her."

With his manic mouth twisted into a writhing smile, he spread his hands. "Everyone to his own theories, Lieutenant."

"What I can't understand, though, is why you're going after me and Ann—Mrs. Haywood. If I were you, Biggs, I'd be staying away from the police, not harassing them."

"Of course," he said, "I don't know what you're talking

about. But let's suppose—just suppose—that I am harassing you, as you say. Wouldn't it be simple justice?"

I decided not to reply.

"You paralyzed my mother and caused her death, either directly or indirectly. Then you—the police, the city, the coroner —you all conspired against me. You had my mother's death ruled a possible suicide, so that I can't collect what's mine. And then you got to my lawyer, didn't you? In fact—"

"It should've been ruled murder. We both know it. You thought you'd still collect for her paralysis, even though she was dead."

"In fact," he continued, "my lawyer now tells me that he won't go ahead with my case unless I pay him some money. *More* money, that is, than I've already paid him."

"So that's it."

He nodded. "That's it."

"Where do you get your money, Biggs? Steal it?"

His only answer was a slow, knowing smile. He was taunting me with a mute, unprovable acknowledgment of the charge.

"Why don't you go after your lawyer? Stick a knife in his wife's pillow if that's what turns you on."

"Knife?" The knowing smile insolently widened. "Pillow? I don't know what you mean, Lieutenant. I'm totally confused."

"You might be confused, Biggs, but I'm not. I see creeps like you every day. You commit a crime. In this case, you murdered your mother. You feel guilty. Not consciously, but unconsciously. So you start playing with the police—daring them to solve the crime. You might even drop little clues or make stupid mistakes. You commit other crimes to keep the police on the hook. Subconsciously, you want to be caught. Because really you want to get rid of your guilt. The only problem, though, is that sometimes a lot of people suffer—and even die —before we catch up with you."

Mock wonderingly, he shook his head. "You're quite a psychologist, Lieutenant." He stared at me thoughtfully. Then, in a low voice: "Maybe I've underestimated you."

"Maybe you have." I rose to my feet and crossed the living room to stand over him. "If I were you, Biggs, I'd pack up my electronic gear and my burglar tools and get out of town. Because if I have any more trouble with you, I'm going to bust your ass. I know all about how intelligent you are, and how you're a scientific genius." As I spoke, I reached inside my jacket, withdrawing a blackjack. "But I've discovered that a lot of you geniuses aren't very tough." I suddenly slammed the blackjack down on the chairback, close beside his head. "*Are* you?"

He didn't flinch—hardly blinked.

"I'm tough enough, Lieutenant," he whispered. "You'll find out, very soon, that I'm tough enough. Because I've been looking for you for a long, long time. All my life I've been looking for you. I've even had dreams about you. Did you know that? Literally, before I ever knew your name or your face—years and years ago—I dreamed about you." As he spoke, his eyes became utterly transparent, revealing a terrible void. His voice dropped to a low, almost hypnotic chant. "Sometimes you'd be just a silhouette—formless, like a shadow. Other times I'd hear you howling—like a jackal, leading the pack. And now, finally, I can see your face. Even when I close my eyes, I can see your face."

Resting his head against the chair, he allowed his eyes to slowly close. "And soon whenever you have a nightmare," he whispered, "you'll see my face, too. For a while, anyhow, you'll see my face. Until, finally, you see nothing." His lips curved gently, smiling. "Nothing at all."

As I stood over him, silently watching his pale face dream-twitching, I realized that I was in danger. This boy, I knew, could do me harm.

I dropped the blackjack in my pocket, turned, and left the house.

Fifteen

I'd just put my revolver in the desk drawer and was riffling through the contents of my "in" basket when my door opened and Friedman entered the office. He stood for a moment with his back to the closed door as we exchanged a long, silent look. Finally he drew a cigar from his vest pocket—as usual. He sat in my visitor's armchair, frowning down on the task of stripping the cellophane from the cigar. He folded and re-folded the cellophane into a small, neat square, which he flipped into my wastebasket.

"What'd Biggs have to say?" His voice was completely neutral.

"He wants my ass," I answered. Then, as I watched him sail the inevitable smoking match toward my wastebasket, I added in a flat, expressionless voice, "You were right. I probably shouldn't've gone."

I didn't want to say it. I didn't really believe it. But I knew that it was necessary for me to say it.

I watched him subtly relax as he blew a slow, self-satisfied plume of smoke up toward the ceiling—as usual. "The older I get," he answered smugly, "the more often I'm right. It's not much consolation for getting old, I suppose. But it's better than being wrong."

We exchanged an offhand glance, confirming the end of the

daylong tension between us. Then, stubbornly, I said, "Still, I think I picked up something we can use."

"Hmm." Another slow plume of smoke rose toward the ceiling. "What'd you pick up?" It was an elaborately noncommittal question.

"Biggs said that his lawyer is asking for more front money before he'll take Biggs's case into court."

"That's good," Friedman admitted. "That means the lawyer isn't sure enough of the case to take it for a contingency fee." He paused, then thoughtfully said, "Where's Biggs getting the money, I wonder?"

"Maybe he's stealing it."

"Yeah," he answered thoughtfully, "maybe he is. Now, wouldn't that be convenient? Assuming, of course, that he gets caught."

"That's what I was thinking."

"As a matter of fact," he continued, "we should've been looking into Biggs's means of support during these last six months since his mother died. I just assumed that Frazer was giving him money, pending the outcome of the lawsuit. And maybe he *was* getting something. But not lawyer's fees. Not thousands of dollars."

I didn't reply, but simply waited for him to continue.

"Maybe I'll leave an hour or so early today and see whether I can find Frazer. It'd be interesting to know a little more about Biggs's finances. I know for a fact that his mother didn't have any insurance or any money of her own."

Still I waited. I watched Friedman's swarthy, heavily jowled face assume a characteristic expression: eyes lazy-lidded, full lips pensively pursed. He was thinking.

"Maybe I'll also make some inquiries around his neighborhood," Friedman said finally. "Those neighbors, I happen to remember, are pretty nosy."

"Thanks," I offered.

"You're welcome," he answered.

"What'd Captain Kreiger say about Biggs?"

"Well, I suppose you'd say he handed down the official departmental line, which he had to do. As I was leaving his office, though, he told me to tell you that if you decided to do something silly, don't get caught. Which applies, I suppose, to me."

"I suppose it does."

"We won't mention my, ah, research to anyone." He drew on his cigar. "Right?"

"Right."

To close the subject, he smoked for another long, complacent moment before asking offhandedly, "How's the Esterbrook case going?"

I took fifteen minutes to outline the day's developments, during which time Friedman finished his cigar.

"It sounds to me," he said, "like we're getting results. I think Fry's got them worried. They're starting to hop around." He frowned. "I wonder what Fry really did see?"

"I don't think he saw much. I think he's trying a little blackmail."

"So let him try. It could work for us."

"I know."

"What's your next move?" he asked.

"I was wondering about a stakeout—at least on the Gaines place. Like you say, they're starting to hop around. To me, Rupert Gaines looks pretty nervous. If he goes out tonight, I'd like to know where."

"Why don't we stake out the Carstairs place, too? And Jonathan Esterbrook's?"

"If you want to put that many men on it, fine," I answered doubtfully. "But it'd take—" I mentally counted. "It'd take six or seven men, anyhow, to do the job."

"How do you figure six or seven?"

"Two each at the Carstairs' and Jonathan's, and two or three at the Gaines house. If we used that many men for every active case we've got open," I said, "we'd be out of business."

"That's true. However—" He coughed delicately. "However, when the captain and I finished talking about your difficulties with James Biggs, he asked me how we're doing with the Esterbrook thing. And he suggested that, consistent with our policy of providing better law enforcement for the rich than for the poor, we should do whatever's necessary to collar the

Esterbrook murderer. Especially while the story is still on the front pages."

I smiled. "You have a way of cutting to the heart of things."

"Thanks." He heaved himself to his feet. "So set up the stake-outs. Spare none of the taxpayers' dollars—many of which, I'm sure, Flora Esterbrook Gaines contributed herself. Meanwhile, I'm going to clear off my desk and then see if I can find Chester Frazer. Why don't you call me at home tonight?"

"Thanks, I will." I hesitated, then asked, "What about Ann? Is someone watching her place?"

"I assigned a car to follow her home from school and then stay with her." As he spoke, my phone rang. Friedman heaved himself to his feet and made for the door, saying, "Call me tonight."

I nodded, answering the phone.

"It's Ann, Frank. Are you busy?"

"Hi." I waited for the door to close behind Friedman, then asked, "Is everything all right?"

"Yes. I just got home. Do you have someone following me?"

"Yes."

"I thought so." Amusement lightened her voice. "They aren't really very subtle."

"They aren't supposed to be subtle, especially. They're supposed to protect you."

"I know. I was just teasing. The reason I called, do you think—" She hesitated. "Do you think we'll be able to go to Marcie's cabin for the weekend?"

Tomorrow was Friday. I'd forgotten. The last time we'd gone to the cabin, we'd left the city late Friday afternoon.

"The reason I'm asking," she said, "is that someone else would like it if we can't go."

"What about going Saturday morning? Tomorrow night might be a problem for me. But Saturday should be all right."

"Will there—" Again she hesitated, longer this time. "Will there be any—problems? Like"—her voice was low and taut—"like yesterday—or the night before?"

I visualized the cabin—a redwood-and-glass cube, hung high over the ocean. Only one road led down to the cabin—a narrow, rutted two-rut track, snaking down the steep slope to the ocean, touching only Marcie's cabin on the way. The slope was covered with thick, low-growing scrub and bracken.

"There won't be any problems," I answered firmly. "And the change will do us good. Both of us."

Reassured, she said good-bye. I told her that, probably, I'd see her that night. I'd be spending the night checking stakeouts. And checking hers would be a pleasure.

I drew a scratch tablet toward me and began jotting down the names of the men I'd assign to stakeout duty.

Sixteen

I'd put Canelli in charge of the Gaines stakeout, and Culligan in charge of both the Carstairs and Jonathan Esterbrook stake-outs.

At about eleven o'clock that night, I drove past the Carstairs house, actually a Victorian mansion divided into large luxury apartments. Because the neighborhood was Pacific Heights, the Carstairs would pay at least a thousand dollars in monthly rent. But, for social climbers it was a necessary expense. In the society columns everyone who mattered lived in Pacific Heights.

Culligan and Sigler were parked in their cruiser, surrepti-tiously drinking coffee from a stainless-steel thermos bottle that Culligan had gotten for Christmas. Catching Culligan's eye, I drove around the corner and parked. Two minutes later Culligan slipped into the car beside me.

"Nothing doing," he sighed. "Nobody's come out all night."

"Did you see them all go inside?"

"Yep."

"Have you got the back covered?"

He shook his head, glancing at me obliquely. I'd given him two men and ordered him to stake out both the Carstairs and the Esterbrook apartments. I hadn't mentioned covering the rear exits. It was one of the unwritten laws of police work that, unless otherwise specified, a team of detectives was entitled to each other's company and the warmth of their car—provided that they could keep both the subject's front door and his car under constant surveillance. The assumption was that, in America, no one goes anywhere without his car. And besides, police work is hard enough, without standing in the clammy cold of a March night in San Francisco.

"What channel are you on?" I asked, indicating the radio.

"Tach two."

"Anything on Esterbrook?"

"He went out to a liquor store about a half-hour ago, then went directly home. His apartment is in the front of the building, over on Telegraph Hill. I've got a rookie on the job, and he's eager." Culligan sighed. "He calls me every five minutes or so to tell me nothing's happened. We're within walkie-talkie range, unfortunately."

I smiled. "We were all young and eager once, Culligan."

"Were we?" he asked bleakly. "Sometimes I can't remember."

"You need a vacation."

"I know. The last vacation I had, I painted my house."

"How's your ulcer doing?"

"Terrible. My next vacation, I'll probably have to have an operation."

"Don't be silly. Don't have an operation on your time, for God's sake."

He sighed again.

"Don't take things so hard, Culligan. You should relax more."

His wan, down-twisted smile was discouraged. "It takes one to know one, Lieutenant. I always figured you took things pretty hard."

"But I don't have an ulcer."

"You're lucky." As he said it, I heard his stomach rumble. He tapped at his beltline. "Excuse me. Every time I talk about it, it starts to growl." He opened the door.

"You should lay off that coffee."

"Yeah," he answered heavily, "I know. You'll be on Tach two, then, huh?"

"Right. And smile, Culligan."

"You, too, Lieutenant." He waved dispiritedly. "You, too."

Canelli had been ordered to cover both the front and back of the Gaines home, including the alley. He'd stationed two men in front and taken the back himself, parking his own car near the entrance to the alley, with a view of the Gaines's back gate. Once or twice, according to the radio conversation, Canelli had taken his walkie-talkie and tried to find a position on foot in the alley close to the Gaines's gate. But each time dogs had barked, lights had come on and householders had investigated. Finally he'd retired to his car. Canelli's bad luck with dogs was a standing squad-room joke.

As I turned onto California Street, still ten blocks from the Gaines house in Sea Cliff, I heard Canelli's voice on Tach two.

"I have someone coming out into the alley—a man. Looks like he's coming from the Gaines house, but it's hard to tell. He—"

"This is Lieutenant Hastings, Canelli," I said. "I'm in the net. Is he coming your way?"

"Yessir."

"How're you going to proceed?"

"Well, I figure that it's probably Fry on his way to Ernie's— even though it's kind of late, it seems to me. That's the bar, you know—the one he went to the night of the crime. And if it's really Fry, then I figure that—" He broke off, interrupting himself. "Yeah, it sure looks like Fry, all right."

I shook my head impatiently. Even on the radio Canelli rambled. I glanced at a street sign. I was at the intersection of California and Sixteenth Avenue, proceeding west. The time was eleven-fifteen.

"It *is* Fry," Canelli said. "He's under the streetlight now, going down the alley toward Scenic Way, where I'm parked. If he's going to Ernie's he'll turn to his— Yeah, he's turning to his left, just like I figured he would."

Ernie's, I knew, was on Twenty-fifth Avenue, a half-block from California Street. I was in good position.

"Can you follow him on foot, Canelli?" I asked.

"Yessir. That's what I figured I'd do."

"Take your walkie-talkie. I'm at California and approximately Eighteenth Avenue. I'll proceed directly to Ernie's and park across the street if I can. I'll get there before he does."

"Hey, that's great, Lieutenant. I'm getting out of the car now."

During the half-minute of silence that followed, I wondered whether Canelli had remembered to lock the cruiser. I instructed one of the two men left in front of the Gaines house to proceed to the mouth of the alley, covering Canelli's withdrawal and keeping an eye on the abandoned cruiser. I speeded up slightly. I knew I might have difficulty parking on Twenty-fifth Avenue.

"He's at the corner of Scenic Way and Twenty-fifth," Canelli's voice was saying, static-blurred. "Am I coming in, Lieutenant?"

"Yes. I'm at Twenty-third. I'll see you in front of Ernie's."

"Should I come to your car, Lieutenant?"

"Yes. You'd better wait until he goes inside, though, before you contact me. Clear?"

"Clear, Lieutenant."

Twenty-fifth was next, a red-light intersection. As I waited for the light, I glanced impatiently to my right. Fry was only a block and a half away, probably. Maybe closer. The light changed, but the approaching traffic prevented a quick turn. Finally, on the yellow light, I completed my turn into Twenty-fifth. Ernie's was just ahead on my left. It was an ordinary neighborhood bar with Venetian blinds at its front window and a single small red neon sign advertising Olympia beer.

I could take my choice of two parking places. I chose the space a few doors beyond the bar. We'd keep watch in the mirrors. I swung into the curb, switching off the engine and the lights. Wearily, I realized that I'd trapped myself into sharing a stakeout with Canelli, possibly until two o'clock in the morning. Originally, Ann's flat was to have been my next stop.

Slouching down in the seat in the detective's classic stakeout posture, I adjusted the side-view mirror. The street was well-lit, and I had no difficulty recognizing Fry when he appeared.

He was dressed with a kind of seedy flair, wearing a trilby hat and swagger-cut car coat. I could plainly see the gleam of his highly polished shoes. His gait was slow and dragging, defeated. As he pushed open Ernie's door, I saw him glance covertly over his shoulder in both directions. Automatically, I checked the time—exactly eleven-thirty.

Two minutes later, Canelli got into the car, placing his walkie-talkie on the seat between us.

"Did he make you?" I asked, still with my eyes on the mirror.

"I don't think so. Why?"

"He was looking over his shoulder."

"Yeah, I saw him do that. But I don't think he was looking for me."

"Who was he looking for? Did you see anyone?"

"Nope." Canelli adjusted the rear-view mirror, settling down. We sat for five minutes in silence, watching the pedestrians come and go. For a Thursday night, Ernie's was doing a brisk business.

"Maybe you should take a look inside," I said. "If he's trying a little blackmail, he might be meeting someone."

"Right." Canelli opened the door. "Do you want me to stay in there, or just take a look?"

"Just take a look, then come back and give me the layout."

"Yessir."

I watched him walking across the street, taking his time. Canelli had the shuffling, foot-splayed, big-bottomed gait of a circus clown. He pushed open the door and disappeared inside. Waiting, I switched my radio to "transmit," and called Culligan. At the Carstairs and Esterbrook stakeouts, everything was normal.

"How long shall we keep on it?" Culligan asked.

"One o'clock, maybe. Let's see how it goes. We can . . ." Canelli was emerging from Ernie's, walking fast. Something was wrong. I signed off and swung the door open for Canelli.

"What happened?"

"He's not inside, Lieutenant. He went out the back door. There's an alley back there. The—" Puffing, Canelli drew a deep breath. "The bartender said he came in and went to the bathroom, supposedly. The bathroom is back by the door, see.

So then I guess he just left. See, the back door is usually barred and now it's not. So that's how they know."

"Where's the alley go?" I started the engine.

"It's one-way—to Clement Street."

As I got underway, I ordered, "Advise your stakeout that Fry's on the loose. Tell them to keep their eyes open. Then call Communications and alert the black-and-white cars in this area. Tell them to keep the subject under loose surveillance. Don't apprehend." I moved the car to the center of Twenty-fifth Avenue, signaling for a turn into Clement. I drove slowly, cruising. "And keep your eyes open for him," I finished.

Already on the radio, Canelli nodded.

Turning into Clement, I saw the mouth of the alley, midway down the block. I nosed the car into the narrow alley so that the headlights swept its full length. Something small and furry flicked out of sight, but nothing else stirred.

"Want me to get out and take a look?" Canelli asked.

"No." I backed up into the traffic flow, drawing a dozen angry horn-squawks, and continued down Clement. I scanned the scattering of pedestrians on my side of the street. Canelli was doing the same on his side. At Twenty-fourth Avenue, I decided to turn left, back toward Sea Cliff. Although Twenty-fifth was a busy four-lane artery, Twenty-fourth was a residential street. The area was the Richmond District, a middle-class neighborhood, mostly flats and single-family dwellings. Twenty-fourth was almost deserted. Teen-age gangs were active in the area, and street crime was high. At the California Street intersection, I waited for the cross traffic to clear before proceeding across.

"He could be anywhere," Canelli offered.

Not replying, I eased the car across California. Again cruising the quiet darkness of Twenty-fourth Avenue, I was aware of a gathering sense of angry frustration. I should have checked out Ernie's in the minute or two I'd had before Fry arrived. I should have . . .

Ahead, on the right, two furtive shadows shrank from our headlight beam. I angled the car toward them. Tensing beside me, Canelli unbuttoned his jacket, then put his hand on the door handle. As I braked, the shadows split, dodging in different directions. Jerking on the emergency brake, I flung myself out the driver's door.

"You take the one on the right, Canelli." And to the fleeing shadow crossing the street I called, "Police. Hold it right there." My gun was in my hand, ready. The shadow disappeared between two parked cars. It didn't reappear. I moved behind a third car, exposing only my head and my revolver.

"All right, come out of there—slow and easy. Hands behind your neck. *Move*."

"I'm coming. Jesus, I'm coming."

"Come on, then."

Head and shoulders slowly materialized. Arms were raised, hands clasped behind the neck. He was small—not more than a hundred thirty pounds. He was Chinese—a young, black-jacketed, blue-jeaned, cleat-booted Chinese hood. There were a half-dozen Chinese street gangs in Richmond. The parents were decent, hard-working, semiaffluent. Their children ran wild.

"Over against the car. Face the car. Spread your legs. Hands on the roof. *Now*." As he obeyed, I kicked his legs apart and slammed his forehead down against the roof of the car.

"Ah—*ow*."

Holstering my revolver, I ran my hands up and down his body. Stuck in one of his boots I found a switchblade knife. I banged his head again, harder this time, and reached for my cuffs.

"I didn't do it, man," he was saying. "Hones' to God, it wasn't me. Hones' to God."

I snapped the cuffs and turned him to face me. Gripping his collar-length black hair, I jerked his face up to catch the street-lamp glow. He wasn't more than fifteen years old.

"What happened?" Gripping his handcuffed wrists, I shoved him suddenly toward our car, hauling him up as he stumbled. Terrified, his knees wouldn't hold him. I could feel him trembling. Down the block I saw the bulky figure of Canelli trotting heavily toward me—alone.

"I said, what happened?" I struck the suspect on the shoulder—hard. His head bobbed toward the spot where I'd first seen him, caught in our headlights. For the first time, I saw the trees and pathways of a small park—a children's park with swings and a merry-go-round.

"We were jus' walking through, man," he snuffled. "Jus' walking through. We—we tripped over him. I swear it, man. He was jus' lying there, bleeding. Hones' to God."

At the car, I shoved him against the fender and gave him his rights. Canelli was on the radio, ordering reinforcements and describing the other suspect. Pocket by pocket, I began searching the suspect.

"Who'd you trip over?" I asked. "Where is he?"

"Man, I don' know him. We were just there, you know—walking through, like I said."

Finishing my search, I handed everything to Canelli: a billfold with three dollars, keys, a Chap Stick, some loose change and a pair of brass knuckles.

"Show me." I pushed him toward the park, gesturing for Canelli to come along. As we approached the park, Canelli explained, apologetically, that he'd lost his man when the suspect had run down an alley and hopped a fence.

"Don't worry about it," I said, jerking sharply on the suspect's handcuffs. "This one'll tell us where his buddy lives." I jerked again, harder. "*Won't* you?"

No reply.

"Where's the victim lying?"

"R—right over there."

"If he's bleeding from a knife wound, you're going to have a hell of a time explaining it to your ancestors."

"Jesus, you gotta believe me. He was jus' lying there, I tell you."

"All right. Show us." As I spoke, a black-and-white car was pulling to a stop behind our cruiser. Another car was rounding the corner, coming fast. "Did you call for an ambulance?" I asked Canelli.

"Yessir."

We were inside the park now; the suspect was leading us toward a small grove of trees in the middle of which I could see a circle of four benches surrounding a sandpile. Peter Fry was stretched out close beside the sandpile.

"Hold it right here," I ordered. Turning to Canelli, I spoke in a low voice: "Take him back and stick him in one of the black-and-whites. Tell the uniformed men to secure the park, but don't come in this grove. I don't want them screwing up the evidence. Call in for three or four more units and the lab crew."

"Yessir." Canelli grabbed the suspect.

"Alert the stakeouts to what's happened. Tell them to stand by for orders. Then interrogate him—" I gestured to the young Chinese hood. "Find out how—"

A low moan came from the sandpile. Two quick strides and I was kneeling beside Fry. His trilby hat lay close beside his head. His eyes were half open, staring up at the sky. As he groaned again, blood bubbled on his lips. I carefully unbuttoned his coat, looking for the spurt of arterial bleeding. All I saw was a blood-soaked torso. I also saw an army-style .45 caliber automatic stuck in Fry's belt.

"Who did it, Fry?"

No response.

I heard the siren-wail of the ambulance, coming fast. When the ambulance crew arrived, I must give up the victim.

"*Fry.* It's Lieutenant Hastings. Did you see who did it?"

Slowly, the pale lips parted. Two ribbons of blood spilled from either corner of his mouth. His eyes came open, fixed on me.

"Who did it, Fry? *Tell* me. *Quick.*"

"All—" He choked on the blood. I slipped my hand behind his head, raising him away from the cement. His hair was sticky and wet. My fingers, I knew, were bloody.

"All—all bows," he whispered.

"What?"

"All—bows. Like Tuesday. J—just like Tuesday. Runs like—like a woman. All elbows."

The siren-wail was a close-by shriek now.

"*The face.* Did you see the face?"

I felt the slippery head move feebly in my hands. He was trying to shake his head. In the street, the ambulance was braking to a stop. Suddenly Fry's scrawny body stiffened, convulsed, relaxed. His head lolled dead in my hands. As I lowered the head gently to the sidewalk, I heard footsteps approaching. It was the ambulance stewards, moving quickly.

126

Aftershock

Withdrawing my hands, I saw my palms covered with blood. Surreptitiously, I wiped my hands on Fry's overcoat. Then, still kneeling beside him, I slipped the .45 from his belt. Standing, I stepped aside, gesturing for the stewards to take over. As I released the pistol's magazine, a fully loaded clip fell into my free hand. Pulling back the slide, I ejected a live round into the sand at my feet. I eased off the .45's hammer, put the gun in one pocket and the magazine in the other, and reached down for the single cartridge.

"He's had it," a close-by voice said. "He's dead."

"Let's send for the coroner," a second voice said. And to me: "Are you in charge here?"

I nodded, identified myself and asked the attendants to try and determine what kind of weapon was used. Then I strode quickly to my car. Canelli had put the Chinese hood in the back seat and was sitting beside him.

"I told you to put him in a black-and-white car," I snapped. "Get him out of here." I jerked my head. "Then come back. We've got work to do."

Waving aside his apologies, I switched the radio to Tach two, then flipped the "transmit" toggle. "This is Lieutenant Hastings. Who's answering for the Gaines stakeout?"

"I am, Lieutenant. Palmer."

"Have you got both the back doors and the front door covered tight, Palmer?"

"Yessir."

"*Tight?*"

"Well—" I heard him cough. "I think so, sir. Springer's where Canelli was, I know. So I—"

"Are you in walkie-talkie communication with Springer?"

"Yessir."

"Find out his exact position. If he's at the mouth of the alley, I want him to proceed to the Gaines's back gate. There's no need for keeping quiet now. Peter Fry's just been murdered. Do you understand?"

"Yessir."

"Tell Springer to watch himself—there's a murderer loose somewhere."

"Right."

"I want you to get back to me as quickly as possible. I want to know exactly where Springer's been for the past twenty minutes. Clear?"

"Yessir. Clear."

"Did anyone go out through the front door?"

"No, sir."

"All right. Get to work. Culligan, are you reading me?"

"Yeah. Just a second—" I heard Culligan talking in the background. He was checking with his Esterbrook stakeout. As usual, in the crunch, Culligan didn't wait for orders.

"Everything's tight, Frank." Under pressure, he used my first name. "Nobody in or out, either here or at Jonathan's."

"Well, somebody went somewhere." I hesitated a moment, then asked, "Is the Carstairs house dark?"

"Yeah. It's been dark for almost an hour."

I hesitated another moment, wincing at the possible repercussions of rousting the Carstairs. But I had no choice. "I want you to turn them out, Culligan. Don't take any crap from them. Find out where everyone was, where everyone was sleeping, who heard what. Clear?"

"Clear."

"Tell them the reason—that Fry's been murdered. If they give you any crap, I want to know about it. Also, I want you to do the same for Jonathan. Your man shouldn't have any trouble with him. But if you *have* any trouble, the same thing applies—no crap. I'll be on Tach two all the time. Okay, move."

Culligan didn't bother to reply. A moment of static-blurred silence followed, then I heard someone say, "Lieutenant?" It was Palmer. From the tentative sound of his voice, I knew what to expect. "Springer's at the back gate now, Lieutenant."

"But he wasn't there until now, is that it?"

"I—yessir, that's it."

"Did he see anyone enter the Gaines's garden in the last few minutes?"

"No, sir."

"Could anyone have gotten in without him seeing?"

"He says there's a chance, sir. A very small chance."

"All right, don't sweat it, Palmer. You didn't do anything wrong. I think you'd better—" I paused, frowning. There were only two people inside the Gaines house now—Rupert Gaines and Charlotte Young. One of them could be the murderer. One of them could have slipped out the gate behind Fry, gone in the opposite direction down the alley, picked up Fry later. If the murderer knew Fry's destination—the park—he could have been waiting, unseen.

Runs like a woman.

I remembered Rupert Gaines yesterday, flouncing down the hallway, swinging his hips. How did Rupert Gaines run? How did Charlotte Young run?

For that matter, what about Jonathan?

And Grace Carstairs—the angular Pacific Heights society matron. How did Grace run?

Was Susan Platt a suspect now? How did Susan Platt run?

I decided that, without supervision, I didn't want Palmer and Springer entering the Gaines house and conducting an interrogation. I ordered them to maintain their positions, never mind the barking dogs and curious neighbors. I would send them reinforcements. As I spoke, Canelli got into the car in the driver's seat.

"What about that Chinese kid?" I asked. "What's his story?"

"Jeeze, Lieutenant, I didn't mean to screw up when I—"

"Never mind, Canelli. I'm sorry I yelled at you. Now, what'd the Chinese kid say?"

"He didn't say anything much different than he told you, as I get it, Lieutenant. I mean, he says that his buddy and him were just walking by across the street, there—" Canelli pointed. "And, as I get it, they saw someone running out of the park— like he was running away from something. That was the kid's first story, anyhow. But then it turns out that they thought they heard a shot, maybe. To be honest, I didn't get it real straight, Lieutenant. I mean, I have to say that I have a lot of trouble talking to these—"

"Canelli. Please. We've got lots to do."

"Oh, yeah. Sorry, Lieutenant. Well, anyhow, for whichever reason, the two of them decided to investigate—the suspect and his buddy. I get the feeling they thought it might've been a rumble, or something. Maybe they were just looking for some action. Anyhow, when they got to the park, they heard Fry groaning."

"Was he lying where we found him?"

"Yeah."

"Did they touch Fry? Roll him, or anything?"

Canelli shook his head. "I don't think so, Lieutenant."

"All right. What happened then?"

He shrugged. "Then we arrived, the way I get it."

"Get the car started, and keep the radio on Tach two. I'll be with you in a minute." I got out of the car and gestured to one of the ambulance stewards. As he was responding, I beckoned for a plain-clothes man who'd just arrived. I knew the detective was from the morals squad, but I couldn't remember his name.

He saved me the trouble. "It's Ralston, Lieutenant."

"Okay, Ralston. I've got to leave here. The lab crew is on the way, and the coroner. Take over, will you?"

"Yessir." He turned immediately away, frowning importantly. He was a young man, eager to take command. The ambulance steward was standing beside me.

"It was a gunshot wound in the abdomen, Lieutenant," he said laconically. "Medium-size weapon, if I had to guess. A .32, say. There wasn't any exit wound."

I nodded acknowledgment and returned to the car. "Anything?" I asked Canelli, pointing to the radio.

"No, sir."

"All right, let's find a phone booth, quick. Go back to California Street and turn over to Twenty-fifth."

"Roger."

As Canelli made a laborious U turn, I checked my watch. The time was five minutes after midnight. Thirty-five minutes had elapsed since Fry entered Ernie's bar. Assuming he'd left the bar immediately and walked directly to the park, it could have been twenty minutes, at least, since the murder. During those twenty minutes, any of the suspects could have reached home. They could have—

"There's a phone, Lieutenant," Canelli said.

"I want you to phone Susan Platt," I ordered. "She lives in the Marina somewhere. Find out what she's been doing all night. Hurry it up."

"Roger." Canelli drove across Twenty-fifth on the red light and pulled to a stop close beside a phone booth. He got out of the car and strode quickly to the booth, searching his pockets as he walked. Now he was turning back, his expression sheepish. Muttering, I took a handful of change from my own pocket, handing it through the window.

"Lieutenant Hastings?" It was Culligan's voice on the radio.

I grabbed the microphone and acknowledged the call.

"It would've been possible for either of the Carstairs to've done it, but not very likely. There's a back service stairway and an alley behind the house. Charles and Grace were sleeping in separate rooms and the daughters were both asleep by eleven o'clock."

"What about Charles and Grace? When'd they go to bed?"

"She went to sleep at about ten, she said—because she was exhausted, supposedly. She said she took a sleeping pill. Carstairs went to sleep about ten-thirty."

"Supposedly."

"Yeah. Supposedly."

"They go to bed pretty early, it seems to me—especially with funeral arrangements to make." As I said it, I was watching Canelli. He was having difficulty, scowling at the pay phone and waving a pudgy hand.

"I was thinking the same thing," Culligan said.

"What about their cars?"

"Buttoned up tight."

"What about Jonathan?"

"I haven't— Wait a minute. I'm getting something now on the walkie-talkie. Hold on a minute, okay?"

"Okay." I rolled down the window and called, "What's happening, Canelli?"

"The goddamn number's unlisted," he said heatedly. "And the goddamn phone supervisor won't—" He pressed the receiver closer to his ear. "Wait. Here's the number now." I watched him writing on the back of his hand, frowning and nodding at the phone. As he began dialing, I checked the time. Almost twelve-fifteen.

Runs like a woman.

Someone had said Susan Platt had the balls. Was it possible that—

"Lieutenant?" It was Culligan.

"Yes."

"It's the same story with Jonathan as with his sister, it looks like. He was in bed by ten o'clock, watching TV. Asleep by eleven, he claims. But he could've gotten out the back. His car was parked on the street in front of his building, though."

"Anyone can rent a car."

"I know."

"Well—" I sighed. "I guess you've done everything you can, for tonight. We can't search for a gun without a warrant. Why don't you go home? I'll see you at the Hall tomorrow."

"Right. Are you going to check the Gaines house?"

"Yes." As I signed off, I saw Canelli hanging up the phone. Returning to the car, he shook his head as he slid under the wheel.

"Whew, that Susan Platt's really tough," Canelli said ruefully. "She was really pissed-off."

"What'd she say?"

"She said that she went to a movie and just got home about a half-hour ago."

"Did she go alone?"

"Yeah."

"We'll talk to her tomorrow." I gestured in the direction of Sea Cliff. "Let's see what—"

"Inspectors Eleven."

It was Communications, calling us on the tactical channel.

"This is Inspectors Eleven," I responded. "Lieutenant Hastings."

"I have a message for you to call 824-4076, Lieutenant." It was Ann's number.

"When did you get the message?" I asked, at the same time signaling for Canelli to keep the car at the curb.

"Just a minute ago, Lieutenant. The name is Haywood. Ann Haywood."

"All right. Thanks." I flung open the door and strode to the phone booth.

Aftershock

A moment later I heard Ann's voice. Her words were muffled by sobs as she faltered. "I—I just got a horrible phone call, Frank. I'm sorry to bother you. I know you're—" She momentarily choked. "You're busy. But I—"

"Tell me what happened. Take a deep breath, Ann, and tell me what happened. Be as objective as you can. Pretend you're talking about something that happened to someone else. Do you understand?"

"Yes." I heard her draw a deep, obedient breath.

"All right. Now, speak slowly and distinctly."

"This isn't—on the radio, is it?"

"I'm phoning from a booth. Now tell me what happened."

"Well, it—it was just a few minutes ago. And at—at first, he spoke very pleasantly. He—"

"Was the voice disguised?"

"No. It was very clear. Very polite."

"Was it a young man's voice, or an older man's?"

"It—it was young."

"All right. Sorry. Go ahead."

"Well, he—first, he apologized for waking me up. He said that he realized I'd been having problems, and he didn't want to trouble me. But he said that he had something that he—he thought I should hear. He said it was a recording."

"A recording? Is that exactly what he said?"

"Ye—yes."

"Go ahead."

"He—he said that he wanted to play it for me. By that time I was wider awake. I—I thought first that he might be a neighbor, or someone, trying to help identify whoever had broken in yesterday. So I was—" She faltered. "I was receptive, at first. Even after the music started, I didn't—"

"Music?"

"Yes. I should have suspected something when I heard it. I guess I *did* suspect something. You see it was—it was Rachmaninoff's *Isle of the Dead*. He was playing it like a—a theme song for one of those old-fashioned radio horror programs. And the voice, when it came on, was like that, too. It reminded me of some of the things Orson Welles used to do. It—it was like Orson Welles reading Poe. Except that it was—"

133

Again she faltered. This time her voice dropped to a whisper. "It was obscene Poe."

"What'd he say, Ann? I hate to rush you, but there's something else I've got to do."

"Well, I—I don't remember what he said. Not exactly. Not the words. But it started out with you, and your—your 'crime,' as he called it. Then he—he talked about you and me, together. That was the worst part, darling. Because, from some of the things he said, I realized that he—he'd overheard us together."

"Could you tell *where* he'd overheard us? Was it in the car? Your place? My place?"

"I—I'm not sure. I was so shocked that I couldn't—"

"Were the voices actually ours—actually recordings?" I deliberately spoke in an official, impersonal tone. Every minute that passed gave Fry's murderer an edge. I had work to do.

"No. It was his voice. The whole thing was in his voice."

"Was the voice on the recording the same as the voice on the phone?"

"I think so. I'm not positive, but I think so. The voice on the phone was much lighter—more friendly, more casual. The voice on the recording was artificial—deep and dramatic. But they sounded the same."

"What'd he say next? After the part about—us?"

"Well, then it got very—spooky. Surrealistic. Listening to it, I remember that I was thinking of Dante's Inferno. It was all about souls sputtering in hell. And he—he described how we'd be punished. Mutilated, really. Sexually mutilated. That—" Her voice dropped to a whisper. "That was terrible, too."

"Is that all? Everything?"

"Yes, except that, after the recording was over, the same light, polite voice came on the line. He said that he knew I'd be 'interested in what the future holds.' Then he hung up."

Still speaking in a clipped, official voice, I said, "I'd like you to do three things, Ann. First, leave your phone off the hook. Second, take a half-hour and write down everything you can remember about the conversation. Especially the part where he talks about us—the part that made you realize he'd overheard us together. Then, when you've done that, have a good, big drink and go back to bed. Remember, we've got two men watching your house. And, what's more, I'm going to—" I hesitated. "I'm going to make *sure* you aren't bothered. So you're not to worry. You're perfectly safe—safer than you'd normally be, as a matter of fact. Do you believe that?"

"Yes, Frank."

"All right. I'm sorry, Ann, but I've got to go now. I won't call you tonight. I won't see you. But I'll talk to you tomorrow."

"Yes." The single subdued monosyllable was little-girl-soft.

I said good-bye to her as tenderly as I could. Returning to the car, I ordered Canelli to drive the three blocks to the Gaines house. Before he could ask about the phone call, I gave him his orders. "I'm going to drop you at the Gaines place. I've got something that I have to do. I want you to call for a black-and-white team. Then I want you to roust Gaines and Charlotte Young. Interrogate whoever comes to the door first. It'll probably be Charlotte. Tell her that Fry is dead and get her story. Get her account of Rupert's movements tonight, too. Her room is in the back of the house. If Rupert slipped out into the alley, she might've seen him. Then question Rupert. Tell him a woman's a possible suspect and see what he says. He might have seen Charlotte moving around. She might've decided to strike a blow for her black brothers. Or maybe Susan Platt did it and Rupert's sweating for her." As I spoke, I took Fry's pistol from my pocket and examined it with a flashlight. As I'd suspected, it was a U. S. Government pistol. He'd gotten the gun in the army. Expecting trouble tonight, he'd stuck the .45 in his belt.

I held the automatic up for Canelli to see. "This is an army issue. Find out if either Charlotte or Rupert knew whether Fry had a gun and whether he was in the habit of carrying it. Personally, I doubt it. I think he went out tonight to meet the murderer, and he was taking precautions."

"I think so, too, Lieutenant."

"Also, find out whether Fry had any phone calls today, or went out during the day to meet anyone."

"Yessir." Canelli pulled up in front of the Gaines house and got out of the car.

As I slid behind the wheel I said, "I'm sorry to stick you with all this, Canelli, but there's something I've got to do. I should be home in an hour. Call me if there're any problems. I think, under the circumstances, you should call for a team to keep this place staked out all night." As I said it, I glanced at the Gaines house. I could see only one light, doubtless a night light. I looked up and down the street. In Sea Cliff, at twelve-thirty, everything was quiet.

I nodded to Canelli, wished him luck, and pulled away from the curb. It would take me approximately fifteen minutes to reach the Frazer house.

Seventeen

The house looked just as I'd first seen it yesterday. The Dodge Dart was still parked in the driveway; the small front garden and porch were still strewn with advertising circulars. From all appearances, the darkened house could be deserted.

Slipping a tire iron from beneath my coat, I stepped close to the front door and carefully inserted the curved end of the iron into the doorjamb opposite the lock. A single strong, steady pull broke the wooden strip of doorstop free. Reversing the iron, I slid the tapered end directly into the crack between the door and the jamb. I glanced back over my shoulder, then leaned my full weight on the iron—once, twice. On the third try, the door came free. A final cautious glance over my shoulder, and I was inside, carefully closing the door behind me. As I stood motionless in the hallway, adjusting my eyes to the darkness, I shifted the tire iron to my left hand and drew my revolver.

I could hear nothing—no creaking of floorboards, no soft scuttle of movement across a carpet. Had he heard the sound of the door being forced? Was he home? Was he . . .

From behind me came a clothing-rustle. Whirling, crouching over my revolver, I heard a click, saw an oblong of light fall across the hallway floor. Someone had shifted in bed, clicked on a bedside light. Motionless, I waited for the creak of bedsprings, the sound of approaching footsteps. I heard nothing.

He was waiting for me.

Walking softly, moving close to the wall, I slowly advanced. At his bedroom door I stopped, listening. Still I could hear no sound of movement. Drawing a deep breath, I stepped quickly into the open doorway, revolver ready.

Naked to the waist, James Biggs was sitting up in a double bed. In his right hand he held an automatic pistol. Resting almost negligently on the counterpane, the pistol was aimed directly at my chest.

His mouth was twisted into a writhing demon's smile. His voice was a devil's whisper. "I could kill you for a prowler, Lieutenant. You broke into my house in the dead of night. If I shot you, they couldn't punish me. All of the men behind you, with all their guns and cars and radios—none of them could help you."

I raised my revolver, sighting directly on his midsection. "Give me that gun, Biggs. Put the safety on, and give it to me."

Still smiling, he slowly shook his head. "You can't make me give it to you, Lieutenant. This is my house. I'm defending my house. This is my mother's gun. She gave it to me."

"Put it down. *Now.*"

He raised his thin shoulders, shrugging almost languidly. I saw his thumb move, heard the gun's safety click. When I saw his pistol disappear beneath the counterpane—and saw his hand reappear—I lowered my own gun, holding it waist-high, angled down toward the floor.

"You called Ann tonight, didn't you?"

"Did I?" It was a soft, mocking question. His round, button-blue eyes danced, fiercely delighted with our little game.

"You know you did, you bastard." I advanced on him, raising my revolver as I moved. Now I was standing close beside the double bed. The muzzle of my gun was aimed at his head. I saw his throat constrict as he tried to swallow. I saw the smile falter and fade. But his eyes were expressionless—utterly empty, fixed on the gun. He didn't wince—didn't protest—didn't draw away.

He wasn't afraid of the gun.

Aftershock

In all my years on the force, I'd seen only two men face a gun without fear. They'd both been mad.

I spoke in a very low voice. "Unless you make a sudden move, Biggs, I'm not going to shoot you. I'm not going to lay a hand on you, in fact. I'm just going to talk to you. That's all—just talk. I know you've been tailing me. I know you've been tailing Ann, too. I know all about it. I know that you vandalized Ann's place yesterday—and that you called her tonight. She's got the message, Biggs. She's frightened—more frightened than she's ever been in her life. And I've got the message, too. I realize that, potentially, you're dangerous. The message finally got through. So now I've got a message for you. And if I were you, I'd listen very carefully because I'm only going to say it one time."

I lowered the gun and raised the tire iron, holding its point just below his chin. He looked once at the iron, then raised his round eyes to meet mine. He still wasn't afraid.

"If you ever come near Mrs. Haywood again, or call her on the phone, or touch anything that belongs to her," I said, "I'm going to find you. And when I find you, I'm going to break both of your arms and both of your legs. I'm going to break them at the joints—the knees and the elbows. You'll be in traction for two months, Biggs. For six months, you'll be in bed. When you finally get out of bed and start to walk, you'll need crutches. Then you'll need a cane. All your life, you'll need a cane." I paused, breathing hard. Then, slowly, I raised the tire iron, holding it high over his head. He was sitting propped against a quilted satin headboard. I brought the iron crashing down on the headboard.

Involuntarily, he moved away from the force of the blow. But his eyes didn't flinch. I saw his lips part. He spoke in a low, almost musical voice. "That's the second time today you've come within a few inches of splitting my skull, Lieutenant. And all because of some—some idea you have that I'm trying to harm you."

"It's not an idea, Biggs, and you know it. You know god-damn well that—"

"First you crippled my mother. Then, because of you, she died. This afternoon, you threatened me with a blackjack.

Now you've got a big piece of iron that you're threatening me with. And you've got the rest of them, too—a thousand men, all behind you. You've accused me of murdering my mother. But now that she's dead, I can't live—all because of you. I can't—"

"*You* did it, Biggs. You killed your mother, and you—you're trying to fantasize yourself out of it." Suddenly the tire iron and the revolver felt heavy in my hands. Suddenly I felt defeated by this diabolical boy with his writhing mouth and round, empty eyes. I realized that I'd backed away from his bed.

"I'm going now, Biggs. But I'm warning you—" I raised the revolver, eyeing him over the sights. "I'm warning you—stay away. Because I mean every word I said." I backed out of the room, then turned down the darkened hallway. I'd gone just a few feet when I heard his bed creak. Turning, I saw him standing in the backlit bedroom door. He was naked. His hands were wide at his sides, empty.

Disgusted, I turned away, holstering my revolver as I strode toward the front door. As I reached the door, I heard the urgent scurrying of his bare footsteps, following me. I turned to face him.

He came close, arching his taut, naked body toward me. His voice was a vicious whisper. "It's her I want, Lieutenant. I know it now. I want her to wait for the phone to ring. I want her to look over her shoulder when she walks—scream when she hears something strange. Because I know that you'll be screaming, too, Lieutenant. And every time you scream, I'll smile. Every time you hurt, I'll laugh. And when you bleed—either one of you—I'll hold my hand out to catch the blood. And then I'll lick my hand. I'll lick it and I'll—"

With the back of my open hand, I caught him full on the side of the face. Arms flailing wide, he flew back flat against the hallway wall. Screaming, he cursed me, daring me to hit him again.

"The next time I lay a hand on you, Biggs, it'll be to break your arms and your legs, just like I told you." I flung open the door and went outside, leaving him naked in the doorway. I'd parked around the corner, and I walked to my car without looking back. But I heard nothing. He wouldn't scream now and attract attention. His screams, inside the house, had been just for me.

And his whispers, too: *It's her I want.*

And then the rest of it—the whole sick monologue, delivered in a low, sibilant whisper while he stood naked, his body straining toward me in the darkness.

In the bedroom, he'd loudly protested that I'd ruined his life. He'd described the crash of the tire iron and the blackjack threat I'd made earlier in the day. In the hallway he'd stepped close to me, obscenely whispering so that only I could hear. Finally, screaming, he'd dared me to hit him again.

It had all been carefully planned—all painstakingly scripted for recording.

As I unlocked my car and got behind the wheel, I realized that he'd recorded the whole episode—everything.

Eighteen

"You had a busy night," Friedman said laconically. As I glanced at him sharply, wondering whether he knew of my visit to Biggs last night, he blandly sailed a ballistics report across my desk. "Fry was killed by three bullets from a .32 caliber automatic," he said, "probably a Walther. Two of the three bullets penetrated the heart. All three shell casings were recovered at the scene of the crime."

"Where, at the scene of the crime?"

He took a half-dozen 8 x 10 glossies from a manila folder and heaved himself laboriously out of my visitor's chair. Arranging the photographs on my desk, he pointed as he talked. "There's where you found him. But there, apparently, is where he was shot—approximately fifteen feet from where he fell." He pointed to a picture of the entrance to the park. "The way it looks to me, he was standing there, got shot and staggered to the sandpile, where he collapsed. The shell casings were found here—" He gestured to another picture. "And powder burns indicate that he was shot at a range of approximately four feet. Furthermore, the morals man you left at the scene turned up two witnesses. Did you know that?"

"How could I know it?" I rubbed my burning eyes. "I just got here."

"They were neckers. Teen-agers. According to the investigating officers, they told a pretty straight story and seemed like pretty good kids. They were parked approximately a half-block away—" He pointed to a roughly drawn map of the area. "In fact, they saw you arrive. And it seems that even though they were, ah, engrossed in each other, they were also aware of Fry entering the park, a few minutes earlier. Or, at least, they were aware of someone—a man—walking from the direction of California Street."

I nodded. "That was Fry."

"Right. Then they saw someone coming from Lake Street, in the opposite direction. He—or she—entered the park just a minute or two after Fry."

I sat up straighter. "That was probably the murderer."

Friedman returned to my visitor's chair, sank down with a grateful sigh and laced his fingers complacently across his stomach. "That's what I figured. Unhappily, the young lovers didn't take a very good look at him—or her. They agreed, though, that it was a 'guy in a long coat,' which is about how Fry described the murderer, if I remember. So, having gotten in early this morning, as usual, I've been applying myself to the Esterbrook case in the early-morning silence around here. And, as usual, I think I have the whole pattern clearly in mind. In fact, I have a theory. Which I'll be happy to relay to you, once you tell me about last night's developments."

"First, tell me what else these teen-age witnesses said."

"They said that this second person—the murderer, as you say—was only in the park for a brief time. Less than five minutes, they said. Then they heard shots, followed by someone running toward Lake Street. The murderer, obviously."

"Obviously."

"Whereupon the two young lovers tried to decide whether to run or investigate—or call the police. Finally they decided to wait and see what happened. They saw the two Chinese thugs cross the street and enter the park. And you know the rest." He waved a hand. "So now it's your turn. What'd you find out?"

As I was reporting, both Culligan and Canelli arrived in my office. When I'd finished speaking, Friedman nodded ponderously.

"Runs like a woman, eh?" Again he nodded. "It all fits with

my newly developed theory." He turned to Canelli, saying, "I'll bet I can tell you what you found out at the Gaines house."

Canelli spread his hands. "I expect maybe you can, sir—especially if you think it's nothing, which it was. Zero. Charlotte Young saw Fry leave and that's about it. She didn't even have anything snotty to say about anyone, especially. In fact, I got the feeling that she was kind of shook up that Fry got killed. She admitted, kind of, that she liked him."

"That's probably because he was a fallen white man," Friedman observed.

Canelli frowned. "What?"

"Never mind. What about Gaines?" Friedman asked. "How'd he act?"

"Well, he acted like he'd drunk himself off to sleep, which is what he said he did—about ten o'clock, according to him. And I believed him, too, because that's the way he smelled—like he'd been drinking."

"Did he seem distressed, would you say?"

"Yeah, as a matter of fact, he did," Canelli answered. "He looked real wild-eyed, kind of—like something was really bothering him."

"It all fits." Friedman allowed his heavily lidded eyes to briefly close. He was lapsing into his Holmesian mood—a posture that invariably irritated me. "Everything is coming together," he intoned.

"*What's* coming together?" I asked brusquely. While Canelli and Friedman had been talking, I'd been thinking of James Biggs, wondering whether I should tell Friedman of last night's confrontation. Of course, I knew the answer—that I must tell him. And the answer rankled.

"I think," Friedman said, "that Gaines and Susan Platt went in together on Flora's murder."

"That's just an opinion," I countered. "There certainly isn't any proof."

Friedman shrugged indifferently. "That's true, there isn't. I'm going by personality types. And I agree with whoever it was who said that Susan Platt is the only one in the whole crew with the balls to commit murder. And Fry's 'all bows' statement confirms it. I think he was murdered by a woman. Susan Platt."

Aftershock

He withdrew a cigar from his vest pocket and deftly stripped off the cellophane. As he began folding the cellophane into a small, neat square, he glanced at me, expecting a reaction. When I didn't oblige, he continued, "If I were you, I'd give Susan a good, brass-knuckled interrogation. Get a court order to search her house and her effects. Really lean on her."

I shrugged. "It's as good a place to start as any. I'll talk to her first, then to Gaines. Then, later, I'll talk to the Carstairs and Jonathan. Assuming, of course," I added acidly, "that Susan Platt hasn't confessed in the meantime." I turned to Culligan. "You don't have anything new to report, do you?"

Sourly, Culligan shook his head. Plainly, he was suffering from loss of sleep—along with the rest of us. I offered him the opportunity to stay in the office and write his reports, which he quickly accepted. Next, deferring to Friedman's theory, I told Canelli to get a court order to search Susan Platt's apartment and remove physical evidence as required. Canelli would get the order and meet me in the field. As I glanced through my mail, Friedman lit his cigar. He waited for Canelli to leave my office before asking casually, "Is there anything new from Biggs?"

I dropped the mail back into my "in" basket and clipped on my revolver. Did Friedman know I'd seen Biggs last night? I couldn't be sure. I only knew that, now, I was too tired to tell him.

"I'm not sure," I lied. "Let me go out and see what I can stir up on the Esterbrook thing. The funeral's this afternoon. If I want to catch anyone, I'll have to get them this morning."

Friedman nodded his solemn approval. "That's good thinking, Lieutenant. I've always found that the day of the funeral is a most propitious time for solving the crime. Especially if it's raining."

I glanced out the window at the bright morning sunshine, sighed, and nodded good-bye.

Nineteen

A phone call to the Gaines Travel Service revealed that Susan Platt hadn't arrived at the office, even though the time was 10 A.M. Driving to her address in the Marina district, I wondered whether she and Rupert had talked to each other on the phone—and whether Charlotte Young would know whether Rupert had received any calls.

Susan Platt's apartment building was a luxury high rise, built to allow each apartment a view of the yacht harbor and the bay beyond. As I pulled up in front of the building, Canelli came on the radio to say that he'd gotten the search warrant. I ordered him to meet me in Susan Platt's apartment.

The legend over her bell button in the lobby read "S. Platt," like the sign on her office door. As I rode up to her fourth-floor apartment, I was thinking of Ann—and of James Biggs. Had Biggs taped everything that happened last night—everything but his obscene whispering in the hallway? Was a copy of the tape on its way to his lawyer—the city attorney—the chief of police?

Anything, I knew, was possible.

As I rang Susan Platt's bell, I automatically unbuttoned my coat and loosened my revolver in its spring holster. When I heard approaching footsteps, I unconsciously tensed. Could she be the murderer? If she'd killed Fry, Canelli's phone call last night would have alerted her. She might . . .

The door opened. Dressed in a dark sweater and slacks, she stood with her booted feet planted wide, looking me up and down with a calm, derisive stare.

"Somehow," she said icily, "I was expecting you." She abruptly turned away, striding into the living room. As I followed her, I watched the taut, thrusting movement of her hips and buttocks, provocative in the tight woolen slacks. She would be exciting in bed. One time, she would be exciting.

"Well?" She sat behind an expensive glass coffee table, crossing her legs and staring at me with cool hostility. "What is it you want, Lieutenant? A résumé of the movie I saw last night?"

I smiled at her and shook my head. "If you're offering the information, Miss Platt, I'm sure you've got it."

"Then what's this all about? Why'd you phone me last night, at midnight?" Plainly, she was angry—barely able to keep her voice even.

"Have you talked to Rupert this morning, Miss Platt?"

"No, I haven't."

"Why not?"

"What'd you mean, 'Why not'?" Her voice was rougher now, street-corner-hard. Her eyes were bold.

"I'd think you might've called him to tell him what happened last night. It'd be the natural thing to do, it seems to me."

"You might've forgotten it, Lieutenant, but his wife's funeral is today. I don't think he wants to be bothered by my problems."

"Are you going to the funeral?"

"No," she answered bitingly. "I don't think it would be quite appropriate. Do you?"

"Probably not." I allowed a long, silent moment to pass as I stared at her, trying to force her eyes down. I was unsuccessful. Finally I asked, "Do you know why we called you last night, Miss Platt? Do you know why I'm here now?"

"I certainly don't. I wish you'd tell me—and then leave. I've got a business to run, you know."

"The reason we called," I said, "is that the Gaines's chauffeur, Peter Fry, was murdered last night. He was killed because he saw the murderer leaving the Gaines house the night of the murder. We think that he might've been trying to blackmail the murderer. We think Fry met the murderer last night, possibly for a payoff."

"Are you accusing me of murder, Lieutenant? Is that what you're saying?" Her dark eyes were dangerous. Suddenly the flesh of her high-styled mannequin's face was drawn into a death's-head of hatred. She was no longer pretty—no longer provocative. She was a girl who'd grown up on the wrong side of town—a fighter.

"We have information that leads us to suspect the murderer might be a woman," I answered quietly. "So that's the reason, last night, that we checked out every woman who might've had a motive for murdering Mrs. Gaines. And that's why I'm here. Of course, you have the right to remain silent. You have the right to appoint—"

"You must be insane," she said, her voice choked with fury. "You must be out of your goddamn—"

"Rupert Gaines stands to profit by his wife's death, Miss Platt. And if he profits, you profit. You'll—"

"What makes you think," she whispered, "that I'll profit? What makes you think—"

"Have you ever been inside the Gaines house, Miss Platt?"

"No. Never. Why should—"

"Have you ever been inside the Gaines's garage?"

Shaking her head in a slow, baffled arc of frustrated fury, she said, "No, I've never been inside their garage, either. Why? What're you trying to—"

"In a few minutes, Miss Platt, Inspector Canelli is arriving with a court order that requires you to let us conduct a search of your premises. I hope you'll help him to—"

Suddenly she laughed. It was a harsh, ugly sound. "What'd you expect to find, Lieutenant? A mask? Bloodstained clothes? A gun?"

"No," I answered, "we wouldn't expect to find anything like that." I looked down at the floor. "What we're looking for, primarily, is what might be in your rug, which we'll vacuum."

"My rug?" Balefully, she followed my glance.

I nodded. "Whoever murdered Flora Gaines had to've

stepped in a mixture of motor oil and a cleaning compound that was sprinkled on the garage floor where she was killed. So the killer had that mixture on his shoes when he left the scene of the crime. And if he—or she—went directly home, there'll be traces of the compound on his rug. Or *her* rug. We'll—"

A buzzer sounded sharply. She sprang to her feet, facing the door. She stood with fists clenched at her sides, legs braced wide—ready for a fight.

"That's probably Inspector Canelli." Unconsciously, I'd risen with her. "Do you want me to let him in?"

"Suit yourself, Lieutenant. But if you'll pardon me, I'm going to call my lawyer." She whirled and stalked into the kitchen. Watching her go, I took a last moment to eye the movement of her thighs and buttocks. From the back, angry, the movement was better than ever.

I let Canelli into the apartment and asked him, in a low voice, whether he'd called for the lab crew.

"Jeeze, no, I didn't, Lieutenant. I mean, all you said was to get a warrant."

"That's all right. I'm going to drive over to the Gaines place. I'll call for the crew on the way. You stay here. If Lieutenant Friedman's suspicions are right, she might try to vacuum the rug before we get a chance."

"What if she wants to leave? Shall I stop her?"

"No," I answered after a moment's thought, "don't stop her. Follow her, but don't stop her. We aren't at that point yet. Explain to her, though, that the lab crew will have to effect entry any way they can once she's left the premises. That should cool her down."

"Right. When the lab crew's done, and she wants to leave, shall I follow her?"

"Why not?" I clapped him lightly on the shoulder. "I don't know whether you noticed it or not, Canelli, but the view from the back's terrific. I'll be at the Gaines's, then Jonathan's, then the Carstairs'. Keep me posted."

"I sure will, Lieutenant."

Twenty

I'd hardly pressed the doorbell when Rupert Gaines opened the front door. He looked almost as if he were made up for the role of the haggard husband, wracked by grief. His Byronesque face was pale and puffy, his eyes bleary and bloodshot. A day's growth of dark stubble accentuated his pallor. Wearing a wrinkled blazer, he stood with shoulders slumped, hands hanging loose at his sides, eyes dull and downcast.

His voice was querulous as he complained, "Susan just called. She says that you're going to arrest her for the murder of my wife and Fry." He raised a hand in a flutter of futile protest. "I—I don't understand it."

I stepped into the hallway and glanced at the empty living room. "Let's go in here, Mr. Gaines."

"But the funeral's today. I—I've got to get ready for the funeral." Nevertheless, he followed me into the living room, sitting in the same armchair he'd chosen when I'd first interrogated him.

"I don't understand it," he repeated, doggedly shaking his head.

"In the first place," I said, "we aren't arresting Miss Platt. We're just questioning her. However, before Peter Fry died, he said that his murderer might've been a woman."

"But why Susan, for God's sake?" Then, sullenly: "Does

this have something to do with Susan and—" He swallowed. "With Susan and me?"

"In a way it does, Mr. Gaines. It gives her a motive."

"A—a motive?" He shook his head.

"She stands to gain by your wife's death, Mr. Gaines. Isn't that true? She's your business partner. And your lover, too. She—"

"But it *isn't* true." As he said it, his head suddenly snapped up, eyes blazing. It was the same erratic pattern of behavior he'd displayed yesterday—first a listless lethargy, then an almost hysterical defiance. "You—you can't accuse her of murder just because we slept together a few times. That's not justice, it—it's persecution. Puritanism. You're trying to—"

"It's not because you slept together. It's because Susan Platt would profit from—"

"But she *wouldn't!*" he shrilled. "That's what I'm trying to *tell* you, dammit. I get ten thousand dollars and the cancellation of whatever debts my business owed to my wife. The whole thing isn't worth more than twenty-five thousand dollars. Are you telling me that Susan would commit murder for half of twenty-five thousand dollars? Christ, she makes that in four or five months."

"I see that you've been talking to Harold Rodgers," I said quietly. "Your wife's attorney."

He blinked. "Wh—what'd you mean?"

"I mean that, day before yesterday when you were arguing with Charles Carstairs right in this room, you thought you were getting a lot more than twenty-five thousand dollars from your wife's estate. Isn't that so?"

"Well, I—" His defiance ebbed visibly.

"At the time of your wife's death," I said, "you thought you were going to inherit hundreds of thousands of dollars. And Susan thought so, too. Didn't she?"

"Yes, but—" He shook his head, protesting. "But you—you're wrong, about her. She's not the one, I tell you. She didn't kill Flora."

"Who did kill her, then?"

For a moment he didn't reply, staring at me with his dark,

sullen eyes. Finally, speaking slowly and deliberately, he said, "I think Charles did it."

"Why? Have you any reason?"

"He needs the money. He's desperate for money."

"A lot of people need money, Mr. Gaines. But they don't commit murder for it."

"I know that. But—"

"What did Peter Fry tell you Wednesday night in this room? He gave you a name, didn't he? He told you who he suspected of the murder. *Didn't* he?"

"N—no. He just told me that—"

The phone rang. Gaines jerked upright in his chair, staring at the phone. But he made no move to answer it. Silence followed the second ring.

"Is Charlotte answering?" I asked.

Gaines nodded. And, immediately, I heard footsteps in the hallway.

"Phone call for Lieutenant Hastings," came Charlotte Young's voice.

"Thanks." I stepped quickly to the phone.

"Lieutenant?" It was Canelli. Instantly, I knew something had gone wrong.

"What happened?" I turned my back on Gaines.

"She got out," he answered, breathing hard. "I'm sorry, Lieutenant. She told me that—"

"What'd you mean, 'out'? What happened?"

"She got out and got her car, and she split."

"Have you got it on the air?"

"Yeah. But I've only got a partial make on the car. I mean, I know it's a red Porsche 914, and I've got that on the air. But I haven't got the license number yet from the computer. I'm real sorry, Lieutenant."

"How long ago did she go?"

"Just a couple of minutes ago. Five, ten minutes, maybe. What happened, see, she asked me if she could go to the can —the bathroom. I said okay. I mean, I couldn't very well say no. And I remembered what you said, that we didn't want to take her in physical custody. So I—"

"Is she running? Really running?"

"Jeeze, it sure looks like it to me, Lieutenant."

"Have you told Lieutenant Friedman?"

"I just finished talking to him."

"Where are you, Canelli? Her apartment?"

"Yessir. The lab crew just showed up a little while ago. See, that was partly the problem. They'd just got here and were all antsy to get started. So then she asks, real nasty, whether it'd be all right for her to go to the bathroom. I know I should have checked the bathroom first, to see where the window opened. But I guess I figured that—"

"Never mind, Canelli. You stay there with the lab crew. I'll take over the pursuit."

"Yessir."

I broke the connection. With my finger still on the button, I turned roughly on Gaines.

"Your girlfriend is apparently a fugitive," I said. "If it turns out that she's guilty of murder, and you gave her any kind of help or information, or warned her that she was in danger, then you're in big trouble. Do you understand what I'm telling you?"

Still sitting slumped in his armchair, blank-eyed, he slowly, dumbly nodded.

"She's in her car, running," I said. "Have you any idea where she'd go?"

Almost comically, his dumbly bobbing nod of comprehension changed to a faltering shake of the head.

"Does she have credit cards?"

"Y—yes."

"All right—" I jerked my head to the door where Charlotte Young was standing. "I want the two of you to get in the back of the house. Get in the kitchen, both of you. And stay there. You're not to use the phone or leave the house—either of you. This is police business—pursuit of a fugitive from justice. If you don't obey me, you'll be obstructing justice. Do you understand?"

Charlotte Young nodded, turned, and disappeared down the hallway. Gaines followed, faltering as he walked.

As I dialed Communications and asked for Friedman, I experienced a familiar feeling of mild irritation. Friedman had done it again. Sitting belly-up in my office, smoking his cigars and theorizing, he'd . . .

"Friedman."

"It looks like you were right," I said.

"I wasn't going to mention it."

"I'll bet."

"Where're you?"

"I'm at the Gaines house. Have you got her license number yet?"

"We *just* got it. Apparently she'd just licensed the car, and the number wasn't in the computer. Anyhow, it's on the air. How long has she been running?"

"Ten or fifteen minutes, I'd say."

"If she's heading north, she's already across the Golden Gate Bridge," he said thoughtfully. "But she might not've had time to make the Bay Bridge."

"Have you notified the Highway Patrol?"

"I've notified everybody," he answered. "The reporters are thick down here because of the Fry thing—the murdered dowager and her dead chauffeur angle. If we don't find Susan, we're screwed."

"Why don't you put the helicopter up? That Porsche will be easy to spot."

"Good idea. What're you going to do?"

"I think I'll get a couple of uniformed men over here to secure the Gaines place, then get in my car. Have you got a channel for the pursuit?"

"Yes. Tach seven. I'll go down to Communications. Maybe, between the two of us, we can catch her in time for the evening news."

By the time I'd secured the Gaines house and gotten into my car, Friedman was calling me on Tach seven.

"I just talked to the sergeant at the Golden Gate Bridge, Frank. We got a break. There was an accident on the bridge approach, and traffic's been backed up for ten minutes. She probably didn't go north."

I started the engine. "Have you got the airport covered?"

"Naturally."

"I think I'll drive in that direction. She's got credit cards. If she's smart, she'll get a plane. Either that, or she'll steal a car. She's not going to get far in a Porsche."

"She might've simply holed up—driven to a downtown lot, parked the Porsche and caught a Greyhound bus somewhere."

"Then you'd better cover the bus stations."

"Right. I'll be talking to you."

I switched off the radio. I was traveling east on California Street, making for the Broadway tunnel and the approaches to the Bayshore Freeway. San Francisco is a compact city, squeezed into the northern tip of a peninsula. The Golden Gate Bridge offers escape north to the half-wild hills of Marin County. The Bay Bridge empties hundreds of thousands of cars a day into the broad, arid Sacramento Valley to the east. To the south, three major arteries carry San Franciscans through the Peninsula megalopolis to San Jose, fifty miles away. Two of these arteries lead to the San Francisco airport. The fastest, most heavily traveled of the two arteries was the Bayshore Freeway.

At that moment, I knew, Susan Platt could be on the Bay-shore Freeway, fast approaching the airport. She could park her car in an indoor garage at the airport, out of sight. She could take the moving sidewalk to the terminal, buy a ticket to anywhere—on the first flight out. In a half-hour, she could be in the air.

Driving with one hand, I turned up the radio, listening to Friedman's laconic orders as he positioned his men for the search. The replies he received were equally cryptic—mostly monosyllabic responses to Friedman's orders. Until the red Porsche was spotted, there was nothing to say. I clipped the red light to the dashboard, but didn't set it flashing. Until I got some word, there was no point in my hurrying anywhere. Friedman was right. She could've caught a Greyhound bus. Or she could still be in the city, holed up. Would she try to contact Gaines? Were there two conspirators? Had they planned the murder together? Or had Susan committed the murder, then told Rupert to implicate him?

The last possibility was the best.

Gaines wouldn't have had the guts to plan the crime. But, once implicated, he wouldn't have had the guts to pull out. He wouldn't . . .

"This is Highway Patrol Unit 83," the radio crackled, "reporting from the intersection of Bayshore Freeway and Sierra Point. The vehicle designated in your all-points bulletin, red Porsche model 914, California license NIF 6248, has just passed this point, proceeding south. One occupant, apparently female. We're proceeding north to the first overpass, where we can reverse direction and take up pursuit."

As I switched on the red flasher and stepped down hard on the accelerator, I heard Friedman ask for the location of Sierra Point in relation to the airport.

"A little over three miles," the Highway Patrolman answered.

I picked up my microphone, identified myself and advised all units that the fugitive was armed and dangerous. Then I dropped the microphone on the seat, forced to use both hands as I careened into the Broadway tunnel. As I drove, I swore. I should have stopped long enough to pick up another officer—a beat patrolman—anyone. I couldn't drive and handle the radio. I couldn't direct the pursuit. As a command officer, I was useless.

At the mouth of the tunnel, approaching the crowded Columbus Street intersection, I hit the siren. The sound obscured new voices on the radio. Through the intersection, barely avoiding a Lincoln Continental, I switched off the siren. Ahead was the freeway entrance, with a clear path.

Over the engine-sound, I heard Friedman's voice as he talked calmly to the Highway Patrol dispatcher. "Have you got anyone in front of the fugitive—between the fugitive and the airport turnoff?"

"No, sir, we haven't," the dispatcher answered.

"Have you got anyone at the airport?"

A pause. Then: "Yessir, we have. Two units."

"Well, instruct them to take up positions on the access road leading into the airport from the freeway. I don't much care where she goes, as long as it's not into a congested area where she can hop out of the car and disappear. If we keep her on the freeway, and box her in, we'll be all right. Clear?"

"Yessir. Clear. Out."

"Frank? Where are you?" Friedman asked.

Pounding into the first long, sweeping curve of the freeway's ramp, I couldn't reply. A few seconds later, straightening the car, I picked up the microphone.

"I'm on the overpass opposite the Embarcadero," I responded, "traveling south."

"Can you take field command?"

"When we get her cornered, I can. But I don't have a driver. You direct the pursuit. I can't—"

"This is Highway Patrol Unit 83," a voice cut in. "We've effected a U turn and are traveling south on the Bayshore Freeway. We have the suspect vehicle in sight. Subject is traveling at approximately fifty-five miles an hour and is within half a mile of the airport. We're proceeding code one—no lights or sirens. She's in the right lane, signaling for a turn into the airport. She's—"

"Are those two units in position at the access road?" Friedman asked sharply.

"We're in position," a voice replied. "We've got the road blocked."

Picking up the microphone again, I cautioned, "Remember, consider the suspect armed. She's a killer." Ahead, I saw thickening lines of slow-moving cars. It was the Army Street intersection, the last traffic constriction before the freeway straightened and widened for the run to the airport, eight miles away. As I swung sharply to the right, hitting the siren, I heard excited voices on the radio. Turning the volume up full, I heard someone saying, ". . . hopped the divider. She's heading back up the freeway, going back toward San Francisco. We're under way, in pursuit. She's— Jesus, she's really traveling."

Cutting in front of a fast-moving convertible, I braked, put one wheel on the shoulder of the road and squeezed between a truck and an overpass abutment. Once past the abutment I was in the clear, accelerating. On the radio, someone said she was traveling at eighty miles an hour, heading north. I was doing eighty, too, going south.

"Let's get some San Francisco cars on the freeway, traveling north," Friedman was saying. "With the Highway Patrol in back of her, we'll box her in and force her over to the side of the road. Let's take her before she gets into the city."

The next overpass, I knew, was miles away. Traveling at eighty, she'd be north of the overpass before I could reverse directions and take up a position in front of her. I pulled into the left-hand lane and braked sharply. When I'd slowed to forty, I put all four wheels on the broad, graveled shoulder of the freeway. Twenty feet of gravel and a foot-high divider section separated the northbound traffic from the southbound. Glancing ahead into the northbound lanes, I saw the flashing red lights of the Highway Patrol cruisers. They were a mile away, coming fast. The suspect was somewhere in front of them. I braked again, braced myself and turned into the divider. The car slewed and shuddered as it bounced up onto the divider, then down. I felt the steering wheel wrench, heard metal cracking. I was northbound, driving in the middle lane. In the mirror, I saw the small shape of the red Porsche, speeding toward me. With the gas pedal floorboarded, I fought for maneuvering speed. As the car accelerated, the steering wheel bucked in my hands. The front end was yawing dangerously. The steering linkage had been damaged, striking the divider. In the mirror, the Porsche was larger. Behind the Porsche, two Highway Patrol Cars were in close pursuit. A third patrol car was coming up fast on the right, blocking escape into the right lanes. My car was swerving wildly across two lanes. I eased off on the gas, fighting for control. If I braked, I'd throw the car into a skid. The Porsche was almost on me now, feinting first into the center lane, then darting to my left. I could plainly see the fugitive, hunched over the wheel. She feinted again, whipping the tiny red sports car from side to side. Each time, I turned with her. Finally, accelerating, she turned to pass me on the left, between my car and the shoulder. I waited until she was committed, then turned sharply in front of her. The damaged steering gear snapped my car into a skid. As my front wheels struck the graveled shoulder, I felt the Porsche strike the rear of my car, hard. Instantly, I jammed on the brakes and yanked the wheel all the way over. Locked together, the two cars were slewing toward a low concrete wall. I felt the Porsche sliding along the side of my car, metal shrieking against metal. Her engine was screaming. She was trying to break free before the wall trapped her. As my foot clamped down on the accelerator, my car gave a final lurch, closing the gap. At the moment of impact I threw myself to the right against my seatbelt, both arms thrown up to shield my head.

Twenty-one

"You're going to have a black eye," Friedman observed. "Do you know that?"

As I eased myself into my chair, grimacing, I glanced at my watch. The time was almost four o'clock. I'd promised to phone Ann before she left for school that morning, and hadn't. Now school was over, and she would be home.

"If there's one thing I like to see in a leader of men," Friedman said, "it's a willingness to take risks. Of course—" He blew a lazy plume of cigar smoke toward the ceiling. "Of course, I'm told that, had you troubled to look up ahead, you'd've seen a platoon of black-and-white cars clogging the Bayshore Freeway. Still, I'm sure it encouraged the ranks to see you risking your life single-handedly." He started another plume of smoke toward the ceiling. "Incidentally, while you were getting X-rayed, I took the opportunity to extract a full confession from Gaines." He sailed a three-page interrogation report across my desk. "There it is, signed and sealed."

Wearily, I sailed the papers back to him. "Just tell me about it, will you?"

"Certainly. According to Gaines, he had no knowledge that Susan was going to commit the crime. However, he immediately suspected her. Apparently they'd already discussed how luxurious life would be with Flora gone. At that point, of course, Rupert innocently believed that he'd inherit a half-million dollars or so. And Susan had no reason to doubt it."

"How'd she actually commit the murder?"

"Gaines claims that she borrowed his car a month or so ago, and he theorized that she must've gotten his keys duplicated. The rest was simple. She merely waited for Rupert to leave her apartment on Tuesday night. She pleaded a headache, as the saying goes—knowing full well that Rupert would do a little bar-hopping before he returned home. Whereupon Susan got her trusty lead pipe and dressed up in a man's topcoat and hat, and drove over to the Gaines house—for which purpose, incidentally, she'd rented a car. She let herself in the back gate, pretended to jimmy it and did the same thing at the garage door. All in all," Friedman said judiciously, "it was a pretty cool performance, especially for a girl."

"When did Rupert first suspect her?"

"The following morning, he says. Wednesday. He phoned her first thing, at her home. Just talking to her, he knew something was up. So they arranged to meet that night. Later, Rupert found out that maybe Fry could identify Susan. That part was coincidence, though."

"Where'd they meet?"

"At the Stonestown parking lot. Susan didn't mince words, Gaines said. She announced that she'd killed the old girl—for them. The old routine. And Gaines fell for it. Instead of blowing the whistle on her, he agreed to help cover for her. He also warned her that Fry could maybe identify her. So Rupert put himself right on the hook—right where Susan wanted him." Friedman shrugged, waving his cigar. "It was a pretty stupid performance, actually. He could have turned her in and saved himself a lot of trouble."

"Did Gaines set Fry up—arrange the meeting at the playground?"

"No. Gaines says that Susan called Fry at the house, anonymously. I don't know how Fry could've been so stupid as to fall for the setup. But you can never figure alcoholics. The smarter they are, the kookier they get."

"What's Susan saying about Gaines's story?"

"At the moment, Susan isn't saying a thing. She's in traction, with a bad concussion and internal injuries. She won't be conscious until tomorrow the doctor says—if then. And by that time, you're going to be at Stinson Beach, taking the weekend off."

I looked at him. "You've been talking with Ann."

"That's correct. I've been talking with Ann. Everything has been arranged." He consulted his watch. "You're due at her place at approximately six o'clock. Two hours from now. She's going to feed you a five-dollar steak and a three-dollar lobster salad. After dinner, the two of you are driving up to Stinson Beach. Today is Friday. You aren't to return until Sunday night. You aren't to report for duty until Monday morning. I'm handling everything—including a twenty-four-hour, front-and-back stakeout of James Biggs while you're gone, just in case."

"I was going to ask you about that."

Friedman nodded. "I figured you were. Therefore, you'll be happy to learn that, in consideration of your recent heroics on the Bayshore Freeway, the captain is prepared to overlook your, ah, indiscretion last night."

I sighed, shifting in my chair as I tried to find a more comfortable position. The muscles of my shoulders and back were screaming. I needed a hot bath.

"How'd the captain find out?" I asked.

Friedman reached into his pocket and produced a tape cassette, which he tossed on my desk.

I sighed again. "I was afraid of that."

"The captain, it turns out, is almost as pissed at Biggs as he is pissed at you. The captain doesn't like the idea of snot-nosed kids intimidating his subordinates. He also doesn't like the idea of the city attorney's office telling us how to run our affairs. In fact, considering that Captain Kreiger is an icy-eyed Aryan type who never raises his voice and always keeps his torso muscles tight, I've never seen him so pissed."

"Does Kreiger know I'm going to Stinson Beach?"

"It was Kreiger's idea. It was also his idea that I, personally, take command of the Biggs surveillance. Kreiger, meanwhile, is in conference with both the district attorney and the city attorney."

"When are you starting the Biggs surveillance?"

Aftershock

"At six o'clock. When you're snug in front of the fire at your Stinson Beach hideaway, you can think of me with my coat collar turned up against the chill—protecting your rear, as you might say."

Twenty-two

I winced as I threw a log on the fire—and winced again as I
sank down beside Ann, stretching out full length beside her
on the floor. She lay propped on her elbows, her chin cupped
in her hands. I turned on my side, watching the firelight flick-
ering in her eyes.

"It's almost worth it," she murmured.

"What's almost worth it?"

"All the—the terrible things that've been happening. It makes
this seem like a different world." Dreamily, she smiled. "I just
had a strange thought."

"What kind of a strange thought?" I touched her hair,
smoothing it back from her temple.

"I was thinking that I wished the boys were here—Billy and
Dan. They'd love this place."

"Hmm."

Quizzically, she turned to look at me. "Just 'hmm'? That's
all?"

"Just hmm. That's all. I like your kids. But I like you better.
Or, anyhow, differently."

Mischief danced in her eyes as she murmured, "*Vive la dif-
férence.*"

"Exactly."

"This summer," she said, "we should try to rent this place for
a week or two. You could have your children out from Mich-
igan."

164

Aftershock

I grunted—partly from a sharp pain in my shoulder, partly from surprise. "We'd have to sleep in separate rooms." I eased myself down on my back, twisting to look up at her.

"Would your children mind if we didn't?"

"I don't know," I answered slowly. "What about yours?"

"Summer is still a few months off." As she said it, she returned her gaze to the fire. Her eyes were pensive now, once more reflecting the flames. I laced my fingers behind my neck, watching the shadow of the firelight on the ceiling and listening to the surf pounding on the beach far below.

We seldom talked about our children in relation to ourselves. We seldom talked about the future—or the past. Because we'd both been damaged by divorce, we seldom ventured far beyond the security of small talk and the urgency of sex. We never talked about marriage—either our past marriages, or marriage in the future. We never . . .

From outside the cabin I heard the faint sound of tires on gravel. At the same moment, I saw a muscle tighten in Ann's neck. She'd heard it, too.

Careful not to appear anxious, I rolled up to my knees. The cabin was completely isolated, hung on the side of a steep, bracken-covered slope that fell directly from a two-lane clifftop road down to the breakers below. The cabin's site was a narrow hillside ledge, bulldozed for additional width and buttressed against rock-slides. The access road was twin ruts precariously carved into the rock and shale.

"I'll see who it is."

She didn't reply, but I felt her anxious gaze as I got to my feet and turned toward the door. The cabin was actually one huge room with picture windows across the entire west wall and half the north and south walls. A pullman kitchen and a tiny bathroom formed the east wall, with a sleeping balcony above. We'd put our suitcases on the balcony. My service revolver was in the bottom of my suitcase. I hesitated, glancing at the steep stairway to the balcony. From outside, I heard the sound of brakes locking and a door slamming. Whoever it was, they hadn't come in stealth. I turned my back on the stairway and walked to the door.

Opening the door, I saw a Marin County sheriff's car.

"It's all right," I called back over my shoulder. "It's the sheriff. I'll just be a minute." As I closed the door, I saw the deputy walking toward me. I couldn't make out his features in the darkness, but he was tall and lanky, and he slouched when he walked. The slack, diffident slant of his shoulders reminded me of Culligan.

"Lieutenant Frank Hastings?"

"That's right." I didn't offer my hand as I advanced.

"Name's Reilly, Lieutenant. Marin County sheriff's office. I've got a message for you. It's from Lieutenant Friedman. Peter Friedman. He wants you to phone San Francisco Communications. Right away."

"What's it all about?"

"He didn't say—except that it's important. You'll find a phone at the Standard station in Stinson Beach. Or, of course, you can use our phone. But that's five miles the other side of town."

I gestured to his car. "Can't I use your radio?"

"Sorry, Lieutenant, but our frequencies aren't compatible with yours. The State Police frequencies are, but ours aren't."

Irresolutely, I eyed the closed door of the cabin.

"How long will it take me to get to the Standard station?" I asked.

He shrugged. "Five minutes or so. It's just a couple of miles."

"Will you stay here until I come back?"

"Sure." He eyed the narrow parking area. "It'll take me that long to turn around. Is that your car up by the highway?"

"Yes." I hesitated, then decided to say, "It's possible that there might be some—trouble. I've got a psycho on my tail, and he's been giving me a hard time. So keep your eyes open."

"Right."

Communications answered on the second ring.

"Just a moment, Lieutenant. I have to make a field connection for you. Hold on, please."

A moment later I heard Friedman's voice, static-blurred: "Frank? Are you at Stinson Beach?" He was talking over his radio.

"Yes. What's happened?"

"What's happened, I'm afraid, is that we goofed. Or, rather, Biggs outfoxed me. Take your pick."

"You mean you lost track of him?"

"That's right," he answered ruefully. "I posted two men at his house, front and back, at six o'clock. One of them was Canelli, in fact. It wasn't dark at six, but Canelli could hear Biggs inside the house and see him moving—or so he thought. Biggs's car was in the driveway, too. I arrived at seven-thirty, just to look things over. By that time, Canelli was getting suspicious. All the shades were drawn, and Canelli was seeing shadows and hearing music and conversation. But he was beginning to pick up repetitions in the shadow patterns. So I decided to, ah, let myself inside. And, Jesus, Biggs rigged up some gadgets you wouldn't believe—an eight-hour tape recording that duplicated the sounds of someone staying at home, plus timers that switched lights off and on, plus a device that played shadows across the blinds to simulate movement. I've never seen anything like it."

"Where's Biggs, in the meantime?"

"The last anyone saw of him, he was leaving the house, on foot, about three P.M. He was dressed in a leather jacket and slacks, and he was carrying a couple of packages."

"What kind of packages?"

"One was about three feet long, and slim. The other was shorter and bulkier." He hesitated. "The slim one could be a rifle, broken down. I thought I should tell you."

"I'd better get back to the cabin."

"Do you need any help? I could be there in less than an hour."

"No. There's a sheriff's deputy at the cabin. I'm going to get Ann and take her to a motel in Stinson Beach."

"That sounds like a good idea. Is the cabin isolated?"

"Very."

"If there's anything I can do for you, call me at home."

"I will. Thanks."

"For nothing, I'm afraid. I'm sorry."

"That's all right." I hung up and walked quickly to my car. Before starting the engine, I looked in the back seat, making certain no one was hidden. Driving back to the cabin along the narrow cliff-top road, I constantly checked my mirror. I saw nothing.

A long, slim package . . .

Could he have trailed us to the cabin? It seemed doubtful. As a precaution, Culligan had followed me as far as the Golden Gate Bridge. And, constantly, I'd checked my mirror. Halfway to Stinson Beach, pretending to check a malfunctioning engine, I'd rounded a sharp curve and immediately pulled to the side of the road, switching off my lights. No one had been following us.

Ahead, I saw the turnout where I'd been parked, I turned off my headlights and engine and coasted to a stop. I would walk down the narrow hillside road to the cabin. Quietly, I got out of the car, easing the door closed. Beside the highway I saw a heavy stick, ball-bat-size. As I hefted the stick I thought of my revolver, still at the bottom of my suitcase. With the deputy on guard, I'd decided against getting my gun because I knew it would worry Ann. I'd made a mistake.

I was walking down the narrow graveled access road, stepping carefully. The terrain dropped steeply toward the cabin, two hundred feet ahead, fifty feet below me. The sheriff's car was turned around, facing up the hill toward me. Except for the pounding of the surf far below, the night was quiet. Except for the soft glow of firelight, the cabin was dark. Built straight out from the steep hillside, the cabin was supported by three tall concrete pillars. The cabin's deck and view windows were fifty feet from the ground.

As I walked down toward the sheriff's car, I constantly scanned the wind-twisted bracken that covered the slope. The bracken was waist-high. A dozen men could lie concealed within a few feet of the road. I gripped the heavy stick tightly as I walked, listening for the sound of movement. The road was leveling. I was within twenty feet of the sheriff's car. I could see him silhouetted behind the wheel, motionless.

Motionless . . .

Dead?

Dropping into a sudden crouch, I dodged to my left, behind the car's hood. At the passenger's door, I raised my head to look inside. Even in the faint light of a half moon, I could see fresh blood glistening on the deputy's shirt front. His head lolled back against the headrest. His eyes were open, staring straight ahead.

Dead.

His holster was empty. His shotgun was locked in its dashboard bracket. If I could get to his keys, I could . . .

Behind me, something scraped softly. Whirling toward the sound, I saw the cabin door inching open. Three steps took me to the cabin's wall, my back pressed hard against the rough redwood. I raised the club as the door opened wider. A quick step and . . .

Fingers appeared on the doorframe—slim, timid fingers. A woman's fingers—*Ann's.*

As I stepped before her, I realized that my throat had closed, choked by a sudden sob of relief. Circling her shoulders with my free arm, I felt her sag against me.

"Where is he?" I hissed. "Inside or out?"

"Outside."

I threw the stick away, pushed her inside and bolted the door. Eyes wide, terrified, Ann was moving away from the door. Her hands were groping blindly behind her as she backed away. Her mouth was open, as if she wanted to cry out, but couldn't.

Without speaking, I leaped for the narrow stairway. On the balcony, I tore at the zipper of my overnight bag, tumbling clothing out on the bed. The gun came last. I slipped the revolver from its holster.

With the weight of the revolver in my hand, I felt the hammering of my heartbeat slacken. A hundred times, I'd gambled with this gun in my hand. I'd never lost—never been wounded, never really been hurt.

Moving quickly in the darkness, I stumbled down the stairway. Ann was standing in the middle of the cabin's large single room, still staring open-mouthed at the door. I left her where she stood. Still without speaking, I moved first to the fireplace. With an unburned log, I scattered the fire. Then I stepped to the couch, dragging it around to face away from the windows.

"Sit down, Ann," I whispered. "There, on the couch. Get your head out of sight—down below the back of the couch."

Dazed, she turned to look at me. I stepped close to her, shifting my revolver to my left hand. I slapped her hard, then caught her as she sagged.

"Tell me what happened," I said harshly, lowering her to the couch. "Don't cry. Tell me what happened." As I spoke, my head was constantly in motion, scanning the room's sparkling black expanse of glass. A narrow deck ran along the north side of the cabin, offering outside access to the larger deck that extended full-length across the cabin's west side. As long as the fire still glowed, we were exposed to gunfire from anyone who stood on the deck. But the murderer would be a target, too, silhouetted in the moonlight.

"Tell me," I hissed.

"The—the deputy was standing beside his car. He—he'd just lit a cigarette. I was watching from the window in the kitchen. And I saw the match. He—he'd already knocked on the door and told me to keep the lights out, if there was any trouble. Th—that's the first I knew of it." Sobbing, she looked at me over her fists with a child's gravely accusing eyes. "You—you didn't tell me."

"Never *mind*. Tell me what happened, for God's sake."

"I—I saw the match. Then there was the—the shot. And he—he hit the hood of his car as if"—she swallowed—"as if he was a—a heavy sack, thrown against it. And he—"

"Was it one shot? Just one?"

"Y—yes."

"And then what happened?"

"N—nothing happened. Not for a while. He fell on the far side of the car, so I couldn't see him. But then I—I saw something move, up on the hill. And I—I saw someone, coming down. He was carrying a gun."

"A pistol? Or a rifle?"

"A—a long one. A rifle."

"What happened then?"

"Then I—I heard him giggling. I—I saw him coming down the hill, and I heard him giggling. That was the—the most terrible part, the giggling. And then he—he took hold of the—the body and dragged it into the car. He—"

"Did you get a good look at him?"

Choking on a sob, she first shook her head, then nodded hesitantly.

"Was he about five feet nine? A hundred thirty pounds? Medium-long blond hair, pale complexion? Wearing a leather jacket?"

As I'd been speaking, her eyes had grown large. Finally she nodded. "It's him, isn't it? James Biggs."

Grimly, I nodded in return. Still scanning the plate-glass windows that lined three sides of the cabin, I reached down for her hand. "Get up."

This time, her reactions were stronger, more decisive. She was coming out of shock. I drew her quickly around the service counter, turning her to face the small window over the kitchen sink. I cautioned her to stand back from the window. From outside, I knew, we were invisible.

"Where's he hiding? Show me."

"Up there." She pointed. "About twenty-five feet up the hill, directly behind the—the sheriff's car."

I pushed her gently away from the kitchen window and turned her by the shoulders to face the plate-glass windows in the living room.

"We're going to keep watch in two directions, Ann. I want you to watch the windows in the living room. He could come along the narrow deck"— I pointed to the windows along the north side—"so watch there, where he's got to come from the parking area. I'm going to see if I can see him up there—" I gestured with my revolver. "Up on the hillside."

As I scanned the hillside for some hint of movement, I began speaking softly. "All we've got to do is wait, Ann. Wait, and keep watch. There's only two ways he can get at us—either through the door or from the decks. Either way, he can't win. All we've got to do is wait."

"Wait?" It was a low, tremulous whisper in the dark.

"The Marin County sheriff's dispatcher is waiting to hear

from the deputy so he can clear the unit. When he doesn't hear, he's going to try and contact the deputy. And when—"

"But Biggs has a gun, darling." Her voice was shaking now. "And he—he's already killed that man. He—"

"I've got a gun, too," I answered quietly. "And I know how to use mine. This is my business. Now don't talk. Just look. And remember what I said. Time's on our side."

As I spoke, I eyed the deputy's car. I could clearly see the dead officer, propped behind the wheel. Why had Biggs done it—taken the time and trouble to drag Reilly inside the car and prop him in a lifelike posture? Why had he let me get inside the cabin without shooting?

Plainly, Biggs had a plan—a carefully conceived, diabolically ingenious plan. All along, we'd underestimated him. He hadn't followed us from the city, yet he'd known where to find us. Now he was outside the cabin, with a rifle—a rifle and something else. A package, Canelli had said.

Time's on our side, I'd told Ann.

But only if Reilly's car was controlled by a dispatcher. In some rural jurisdictions, I knew, there was no dispatcher. If there was trouble, a sheriff's deputy called for the state police. Otherwise, he took the car home at the end of his shift and went to bed.

I moved to my right, eyeing the fifteen feet that separated the cabin door from Reilly's car. If Biggs was still where Ann had seen him, up the hillside, I could probably get inside the car without exposing myself to fire. If I kept low and moved fast, I could probably make it. I could leave the car door open. Crouching down inside the car, I could call the state police while I covered the only two entrances to the cabin—the door, and the narrow deck running along the north side of the cabin. I could . . .

Glass shattered behind me.

Whirling, crouched over my revolver, I saw sparkling shards still in midair. Through the shrillness of Ann's screaming I heard the last silvery tinkle of glass striking the living room floor.

I grasped Ann's shoulder, turning her toward the small kitchen window. "Keep watch there. *Don't watch me.*"

Aftershock

I leaped into the center of the living room, crouching behind the couch to face the shattered window. From the darkness outside, I heard the sudden sound of laughter.

"That was just a rock, Lieutenant. Did it scare you?"

The window he'd broken was the first of three windows on the north side—the window closest to the parking area. Yet, from the parking area, the ground sloped steeply down. Twenty feet, at least, separated the shattered window from the ground beneath. Had the rock come from the ground below the window—or from the parking area?

Crouching, I moved to the north wall, beside the broken window. I must keep him talking, to fix his position.

"Come up on the deck where I can see you, Biggs. Leave the rifle behind. Give it up."

"Give it *up*?" The last word was a chirp of manic delight. "After I've worked so hard, you want me to give it *up*?"

The next window shattered, exploding glass fragments all around me. Exposing only my head, revolver ready, I quickly stepped clear of the wall, scanning the ground outside.

"Either give up, or I'm coming to get you, Biggs."

"I doubt that, Lieutenant. I doubt that very much. You might, if you didn't have your girlfriend to worry about. It might be very interesting if you did. Because I can see both the back door and the deck from here, Lieutenant. And I've got a rifle. Did you know that?"

"I don't care whether you've got a machine gun, Biggs. You can't hit a moving target at night. And once I get outside in the underbrush, I'm as good as you are. Better. I've had a lot of practice in this, Biggs. You're playing my game."

I heard him giggle. "How about *two* moving targets, Lieutenant? Do you think I can miss both of you?"

Forcing myself to match his bantering tone, I said, "Ann's not coming out, Biggs. Just me."

"I think you should wait, Lieutenant, until you see what I've got planned for you. Because when you see, you might want to change your mind. You . . ." He began to giggle.

His voice was coming from the hillside to the north of the cabin. With two or three men—with lights and shotguns, I could take him.

At the thought, I felt the beginning of panic. *You're playing my game*, I'd said. But I played with all the men and all the guns and all the support I needed. I'd never taken a killer by myself. I'd never faced a gun without men behind me. I'd never . . .

Through the shattered windows, I could hear the rustle of underbrush. He was moving to his left—up the hill directly behind the cabin where Ann had first seen him. In the faint moonlight, I could see the underbrush move. I raised my revolver, sighting on the movement.

Should I shoot—hope for a lucky hit?

I always carried my gun with the hammer on an empty chamber. I had only five shots. I had no spare ammunition with me. I'd left my handcuffs and spare ammunition in my dresser drawer at home. My revolver was a belly gun with a two-inch barrel. Beyond twenty-five feet, the gun was almost useless. I lowered the revolver, hesitated, then walked to Ann. She was still looking out the back window, as I'd told her. I touched her shoulder and felt her tremble.

"Do you see anything?" I whispered.

I felt her shake her head.

"Are you—going out?" she asked.

Unable to decide, I shook my head. I was standing close beside her, searching the steep hillside for movement.

You might change your mind, he'd said.

And then he'd giggled.

What was his madman's plan? What else had he brought with him, besides the rifle? What was in the other package? Did he . . .

Behind the car, a figure moved. An arm flashed in the darkness, throwing something. I hurled Ann to the floor as the window shattered above us. A fist-size rock struck the counter behind me, bounced and hit me on the shoulder. Instantly, revolver raised, I jumped up. He'd disappeared in the bracken. But if he remained where he was, I could dodge out of the door, gain the cover of the deputy's car and then disappear into the underbrush. I could stalk him through the bracken. The odds were even. Either I found him and killed him, or he killed me—then Ann. Either that, or . . .

Aftershock

A tiny flame flickered on the hillside. I heard his giggle, then saw the flame leaving the ground, arching through the darkness. Trailing a burning wick, a bottle was coming slow-motion toward me, tumbling end-for-end as it fell. I heard myself swearing—heard the bottle strike wood—heard the bottle shatter. Flaming gasoline exploded outside the window.

"That one's for the door, Lieutenant," he was screaming. "This one's for the deck."

Above the leaping fire, I saw the arching trail of another tiny flame. I felt the thud of another bottle, heard glass shatter, saw the close-by bracken brightly lighted. Already, fire was curling under the door—running in rivulets into the cabin.

"That's two, Lieutenant," he shrilled. "I have two more. Are you ready?"

Screaming, Ann threw herself on me. Over and over, she called out my name. I gripped her shoulder with all my strength, thrusting her away from me. I pushed her toward the living room. She staggered, fell to her knees.

"Get upstairs," I shouted. "Get the bedclothing—the sheets. Knot them and take them to the deck. Hurry, for God's sake."

She staggered to her feet, stood swaying as she stared at me with terrified eyes. Then, as if she were breaking free from restraining hands, she wrenched herself toward the stairway.

I ran to the narrow deck on the north side and looked out through the shards of shattered glass. The entrance to the deck was blazing, a spreading pool of flame. I could never get through—not without catching my clothing afire, the perfect target for his rifle.

I crouched down behind the wall of flames and moved to the railing. The ground below, illuminated by the fire, was twenty feet away, my only chance. Once free of the fire, safe in the darkness and concealed in the underbrush, I could hunt him down—protect Ann as she escaped.

I thrust my revolver into my belt, buttoned my jacket around it and grasped the railing with both hands. I rolled over the railing, held on for a moment, then dropped. As I struck the ground my left leg buckled. I was lying flat, concealed in the underbrush. I rose to my knees, searching the darkness for some sign of Biggs. But I was too far down the hill to see the spot where he lay concealed. As I crawled ahead, pain seared my left ankle. I grasped at branches with both hands, pulling myself up the slope—pushing with my right leg, dragging my left. As I crawled, I could feel the heat of the fire close beside me. This time, rising on my knees, I could see the spot where I'd last seen him. I steadied myself, felt for my gun, found it, drew it from my belt. At that moment, another tiny flame flickered on the hillside, fifty feet away. It was a match, moving toward the rag of a wick. I gripped the revolver with both hands, drew back the hammer. I held my breath as I sighted on the match-flame. It was an impossible shot. Even with a target pistol, the shot was impossible in the darkness. As I sighted, the tiny flame grew brighter. The wick was igniting. He would hold the bottle for a moment, to let the wick catch before he threw the gas-filled bottle. I fired—cocked the gun—fired again. The bottle was in the air, tumbling, striking the roof of the cabin. Flame spilled down from the roof, dripping into the side wall's solid sheet of fire.

I heard the shriek of his laughter from up the hill. To my right, I saw a flicker of movement. Ann was crouched on the deck—as I had crouched, keeping down below the roaring flames, out of sight. She was tying a sheet around the railing, throwing the knotted sheets over the side.

I half rose, involuntarily about to call to her. I'd meant for her to go off the far end, even though the drop was longer, more dangerous. Here, close to the hill, Biggs would see her dangling above the ground. He would . . .

The sound of his laughter was louder. Turning, I saw the flare of another match as it moved close to the wick. It was his last gas bomb—my last chance. I had three shots left—two for the bottle, one for Biggs. I aimed—fired—missed. The wick was flaming. As I cocked my revolver, his arm drew back the bottle.

The muzzle of my gun kicked up, momentarily obscuring the bottle. Behind the black shape of the muzzle, something sparked. Suddenly flame spilled in the darkness. In the next instant a blazing figure staggered down the hillside. Burning bits of his clothing snagged on the underbrush, leaving a smoldering trail behind. As he ran, he screamed. Tumbling the last few feet, he fell full-length on the graveled parking area. I saw his blazing body convulse, then lie still. I realized that he was no longer screaming.

On my hands and knees, I thrust my revolver in my belt and turned toward Ann as she climbed the hill toward me. In the distance I heard the wail of a siren. Beside me the bracken was on fire.

When Ann reached me, I rose unsteadily, balancing on my right foot. Together we'd climb up to safety from the flames.

Twenty-three

Friedman waited for the nurse to leave the room, then lit his cigar. He shook the match out, looked at it reflectively for a moment, then dropped it carefully into an ashtray—all the while covertly eyeing me.

I smiled—wearily.

"Jesus," he said, leaning back in his chair and eyeing me critically. "I was right about that black eye, In fact, you're a mess."

"The eye," I said, "is the least of my problems."

"If you're referring to the ankle," he said, "that's *our* problem, it turns out. Mine, as well as yours."

"Why?"

"Because the captain has decided," he said dolefully, "that until you're out of your cast, I'll have to handle the field assignments while you sit comfortably at your desk."

"Cheer up. Maybe you'll get some publicity. You're always griping about me getting my picture in the papers. Now it's your turn."

He shook his head. "I'm outgrowing vanity, I'm afraid. I'm forty-six years old, and I'm fat. I've got other problems besides my image." He drew on his cigar. "How's Ann?"

"She's fine. She just left, as a matter of fact. She asked me to thank you, for coming to get us last night." I paused, then added, "I guess I didn't thank you, come to think about it."

"Don't give it a thought. Incidentally—" He dug in his vest pocket, producing something cigar-size, which he tossed on my bed. "If you're wondering why Biggs was waiting for you at Stinson Beach, there's your answer."

I picked up a metal tube about eight inches long, tapering from a quarter of an inch to about an inch. It was a "spike mike," designed to be inserted into a wall through a hole bored from the outside.

"Where'd you find this?"

"I found it sticking in the wall of your apartment, Lieutenant. Right near where you keep your phone. Need I say more?"

Remembering the conversations I'd had with Ann about the weekend at Stinson Beach, I ruefully shook my head.

"Then I'd better be going. From here, I plan to go to the county hospital, where Susan Platt is ready to be interrogated. Well—" He waved his cigar as he turned to the door. "I'll see you tomorrow. Provided, of course, that I'm not out in the field, risking my neck in the cause of justice."

As the door closed behind him, I glanced down at the floor. An inch-long cigar ash lay just inside the door.

About the Author

COLLIN WILCOX was born in Detroit and educated at Antioch College. He's been a San Franciscan since 1949 and lives in a Victorian house that he is "constantly remodeling, with the help of two strong sons." In addition to writing a book a year, Mr. Wilcox designs and manufactures his own line of decorator lamps and wall plaques.